MW00955612

MURDER OF CROWS

Cover design by Susan Gorick

If it takes a village to raise a child, it must take an entire country to raise a book. A special thanks to everyone who read and suggested changes to improve Murder of Crows long after I thought it was perfect: Roy, Toni, mom and dad, Sandra, Emily, Julie, Kristin, Julia, Mallory, and the one critique partner who literally ripped the story apart and forced me to start over.

And, of course, a very special thank you to Les - he thought the story was perfect from the start.

Chapter 1

Liam sighed, blowing his dark hair out of his eyes, as he watched the trees zoom by from the crowded backseat of the family car. Surrounded by bags filled with groceries for the new house as well as pillows and sleeping bags the family needed until the moving truck delivered their furniture, Liam had nowhere to look but at the pine trees as the car zipped past. The pounding rain streaked the window, making the day gloomier. He rested his head against the cool window, still in shock his family had left the only home he'd ever known and the only friends he'd ever had. He'd overheard his parents talking about the possibility of leaving Florida so his dad could find work as a park ranger, but he never thought it would ever happen.

"Hey, Liam, if you look between the trees you can catch a glimpse of the new house," his mom said from the front seat. "Well, it's a very old house. It has so much character and charm. If the house could talk, imagine the stories it would tell about the lives of the people who have lived here."

Liam could tell from her voice that she was excited about moving into the ancient farmhouse, but he was still upset and wouldn't allow himself to get caught up in his mom's enthusiasm.

As the tree line broke, Liam glanced over and caught sight of the old farmhouse staring at him, sending chills down his spine.

"It's creepy. It's gotta be haunted." Liam looked away from the ancient house and focused on his iPod, trying to shake the disturbing feeling he got from looking at it.

"Oh, it is not," his mother scolded. "You're just upset we moved. Everything's going to be great here. Promise me you'll be open minded. Please?"

Liam pulled his ear buds out, still hearing the bass thumping. "I just don't see why we had to leave St. Augustine for some little backwoods Georgia town. Nobody has ever heard of Mathisville it's so small. Is it even on a map anywhere? Really?"

"Liam, we've been through this a thousand times," his mother warned, not wanting to argue about the move again.

"Actually, the house does kinda look like something you'd see in a horror movie," his dad agreed, pushing up his glasses.

His mom dropped her head and sighed. "You both watch entirely too much television. It looks gloomy and run-down because it's been neglected for the last few years. Once we get a fresh coat of paint on the house it won't look quite so..."

"Creepy?" Liam finished the sentence for his mother.

"Liam, be open minded, remember," his mother begged. Liam put his ear buds back in and cranked his music louder, attempting to drown out his parents' voices.

The rain dropped to a drizzle while Liam kept his eyes on the tree line, scanning for a break in nature. He was curious to see if the house would give him chills the second time he saw it. When the trees cleared, the car slowed in order to make a sharp turn, and pulled onto the long driveway. When it was built the stone wall must have made an impressive entrance, but time and neglect took any sense of the extraordinary away. Half the oak trees were dead and the other half were in such desperate need of pruning that the limbs dipped to the ground, covered in leaves and vines.

Liam's eyes went to the front of the house. The white two-story farmhouse was at least twice the size of their old small beach house. The second story had two large dormer windows in front, making it appear as if the house had wide eyes that were watching the new family approach. The paint was flaking off, like a snake trying to shed its milky skin. The picket fence surrounding the yard was missing wooden slats, making the sinister house seem to grin with holes in its smile.

Frightening, ominous thoughts of haunted houses and mass murders exploded in Liam's head, screaming something horrible, something evil had happened there. He couldn't shake the image of bloodied, dead bodies scattered throughout the house. Goose bumps popped up all over his arms. Seeing the house was just as disturbing the second time.

A shadow in the upstairs window caught his attention. As he watched, it darted out of sight, disturbing the blinds.

Liam sat up straight, yanking his ear buds out again.

"Did you guys see that?"

"See what, son?" His dad asked.

"In the window. I saw it for a second, and then it moved. See? Right there. Upstairs. The blinds are still moving."

"Oh, I'm sure it's just the air conditioning turning on. I asked the realtor to turn it on a few days ago to help get rid of the musty, stale smell. I'm sure that's it. These old houses aren't built air tight, so things tend to shift and move when there's any kind of breeze."

"No. I know I saw something moving past the window. It wasn't the blinds, I swear!"

"Come on, Liam." Mom turned to face him, resting a tanned arm on the back of the front seat. "Maybe your mind's a bit too open now."

The hairs on the back of Liam's neck stood, brushing the neckline of his t-shirt. He still felt someone was watching them. It was creepy. He glanced at the upstairs window again. Nothing. He licked his lips, tasting the saltiness of sweat beading.

As the car slowed to a stop in front of the rundown picket fence, the sky opened up, the light drizzle becoming a pounding downpour again. Even though the family sat in their car thirty feet away, the sheets of rain blocked the house from view.

"Great." Liam yelled, over the drumming of the rain. "Not only are we moving into a haunted house, but we have to do it in the rain."

The family dashed into the house, deciding to leave their groceries and boxes with their sleeping bags and pillows in the car until the rain let up a little.

"Whew! That storm came out of nowhere," his mom said, shaking the rain out of her short, curly hair. "This afternoon rain makes it feel as if we never left Florida."

"We never should have," Liam mumbled.

"Anyway," his dad attempted to change the subject, "let's check out the new house."

The family walked around the house, investigating each room down to the cobwebbed corners. Liam pointed out old water damage, peeling wallpaper, and anything else he felt would show it was a bad decision to move here. Ignoring him, Mom decided where to place furniture and hang pictures, which rooms needed to be gutted and redone, and which rooms they could move into right away. When they finished the tour of the upstairs and picked out the rooms which were in the best condition, the rain had slowed back to a light drizzle. Liam and Dad unpacked the car.

As Liam trudged up the stairs carrying his sleeping bag and pillow in one hand and his trusty baseball bat which was always in his bedroom when he slept ever since Little League, he saw something dark and shadowy dart into one of the rooms. He hesitated a split second before he chased the shadow into the empty bedroom, and flipped on the light switch with his elbow. Nothing. He searched everywhere but the room was just as empty as it had been when he chose it for his bedroom. Still, he couldn't shake the creepy feeling he was not alone in the room. His feet were frozen to the floor. He wasn't able to move if he wanted to. His chest tightened, making him gasp for breath.

Something, someone was watching him.

"Is anyone in here?" Liam whispered.

As if to answer, the old air conditioning unit kicked on again and the dusty window blinds moved in response to the sudden blast of cold air.

Liam looked at the blinds rocking in the window and realized this was the same room he had been looking at from the outside when he saw the shadow dart past the window. He dropped his backpack to the floor and dashed downstairs. Maybe he should have picked a different bedroom.

"Has anyone seen my keys?" Dad yelled up the stairs. "I can't seem to find them anywhere." As soon as the words were out of his mouth, the smoke alarms started screaming.

Chapter 2

It seemed as if the house was alive, first sounding the alarm in the kitchen, then the one in the family room, the one in the stairwell, and finishing with the two alarms upstairs. It was as if someone was sprinting from room to room, hitting the alarm test buttons on the way. But the alarms just stayed on, blaring their warning.

Liam and his mother raced down the stairs.

"What's going on?" Mom yelled, trying to be heard over the wailing alarm. "I don't smell any smoke."

"My guess is the batteries are going bad."

"All of them," Liam asked, "at the same time?"

"Well, if they were all changed at the same time, it stands to reason they'd all go bad at the same time," Dad said, always thinking logically.

"It just seems odd they'd *all* go bad at the same time," Liam yelled to be heard over the blaring alarms.

"Who cares why it's happening, just take the batteries out and make it stop," Mom said, covering her ears.

Without warning, the alarms stopped. All of them. At the same time. The family was speechless, staring at each other in the eerie silence.

"What just happened?" Mom whispered.

"I guess the batteries died," Dad shrugged his shoulders, not concerned in the least all the alarms had just stopped instantaneously. "Liam, go get something to stand on and help me take the batteries out."

Liam grabbed a box and returned to the entry way.

"Not that one," his mom said, snatching the box and moving it back to the safety of the living room. "That's my genealogy box."

Liam sighed, heading into the kitchen and grabbed the small stool his mom never seemed to be without. He placed it under the first alarm, and hopped up. He grabbed the smoke detector, tugging it violently. The entire alarm dropped from the ceiling, into his hand.

"Sorry Dad. I guess I don't know my own strength sometimes," Liam joked, handing the alarm to his dad.

"It's alright, Superman," Dad replied. "Just hand the alarm over so no one else gets hurt." Dad finished in his best wise-guy impression. Mom rolled her eyes at them, but the tension in the room was gone.

"I'll replace the batteries," she said, taking the alarm away from her husband. "You two yahoos keep working on the rest before they go off again."

Liam and his dad were halfway across the room, heading for the next alarm, when they heard his mom's voice, "Uh, John. Come here and take a look at this. Now, please."

They turned to see what was causing his mom's voice to come out higher pitched and squeakier than normal. She showed them both halves of the open smoke alarm. No battery. The battery wires were just dangling in the empty compartment.

"The battery's missing. How could the alarm have gone off?" She asked them.

"Maybe it was hard-wired?" Dad scratched his head, still trying to find a logical explanation.

"Look at it," Mom demanded. "It's not attached to the ceiling. I'm holding the entire thing in my hands." She was beginning to shout, her words were coming out rapid and clipped. "Look at the ceiling. There aren't any wires." Her skin was pale and her eyes were wide with panic.

Both Liam and his father looked up at the smooth ceiling where the smoke alarm had been stuck. She was right; there weren't any wires hanging from the ceiling that could have been hard-wired into the alarm.

"The alarm went off without a battery," his mother whispered. Her eyes were moist as if she were going to burst into tears any second.

"Maybe that one wasn't going off. Maybe we heard all of the others going off in the house and just assumed that one was too," his father suggested. "It's possible."

"Dad," Liam said, dropping his voice to a stage whisper, "that was the one right above our heads. We had to yell to talk to each other. Remember?"

"Then I don't know what's going on, son," Dad said, adjusting his glasses as he always did when he was nervous or uncomfortable. "I just don't know."

Without another word, Liam and his father went to check all of the other smoke alarms in the house, leaving his mother staring at the alarm in her hands.

Every alarm in the house was the same: no battery, and no wires to hard-wire them into the house's electrical system.

*****

Liam lay wide awake on the hardwood floor in his sleeping bag. His eyes burned with exhaustion, but he couldn't sleep. His thoughts jumped around, reflecting on the move and everything else that had happened during the day.

After tossing and turning for what felt like hours, he thought he heard whispered voices. More than one. His heart started pounding. Even though the voices seemed close, he couldn't make out what they were saying; the voices were distorted and muffled. He broke out into a cold sweat. Part of him wanted to burrow deeper in his sleeping bag and zip it up over his head, thinking if he couldn't see anything, it couldn't see him either. But the other part of him really needed to pee.

His bladder outweighed his desire to stay hidden. Sitting up, and straining to pinpoint where the disembodied voices were coming from, he untangled himself from his sleeping bag and crept around his room, willing the voices to become clearer, trying to make out what they were saying. Pacing past the door, he realized he'd heard those voices before: his parents. If he stood right beside the air vent, he could hear their conversation as clearly as if he were standing in their bedroom with them.

Liam grinned. What a great way to eavesdrop. He could hide in the safety of his room, yet still hear what his parents were saying. That might come in handy one day. His grin faded, hearing his mom's panicked tone. Forgetting he was heading to the bathroom, he wondered what had his mom so worked up.

"What have we gotten ourselves into?"

"You know what we have here. You heard about them all the time when we lived in St. Augustine. Shoot, you even gave ghost tours for a little while. What we have here is a mischievous little ghostie!" His dad said, seeming to make jokes at his mom's discomfort.

"But John, what if it's not the fun, garden variety ghost who just likes to play tricks? What if it's an evil ghost who wants to kill us? Or a demon like in those Paranormal Activity movies you like to watch? What I'm worried about is, are we safe here?"

"Of course we are, Darla. I think if there were an evil spirit in here it would have written messages in blood on the walls. It wouldn't have just set off the smoke alarms. That was a harmless prank."

"What about your keys? We still haven't found those."

"Yes, but we haven't found them stuck in our chests yet either. They'll turn up. I'm telling you, Honey, these are just pranks. Nobody's lived in this house for almost two years. Whoever our ghost is will just have to get used to sharing the house again. There's nothing to worry about."

"I hope you're right. Wait! Did you hear that?"

"No, what did it sound like?"

"Rumbling. I think it's coming from downstairs."

Liam heard the deep concern in his mom's voice and threw open his bedroom door at the same time as Dad, both looking down the hallway. Their heads spun as they turned and looked at one another. They both noticed a strong smell of coffee, wafting up from the kitchen.

"Did you start the coffee pot?" His father asked, peering back into the bedroom at his wife, nervously readjusting his glasses.

"No. And I forgot to set the automatic timer for tomorrow morning too, so it shouldn't be running," she replied.

"Well, someone's making coffee. Liam, did you do it?"

"Yeah, I decided out of the blue, I'd start drinking coffee at midnight." Liam rolled his eyes.

"Well, son, let's go down there and check out our late night coffee drinker."

Liam grabbed his baseball bat he'd always kept by his bedroom door, in case he ever needed to check out strange noises in the middle of the night. Falling in behind his dad, they crept down the stairs, one at a time. Pausing when they reached the bottom, the coffee pot rumbled again, making them jump. Liam stayed close behind his dad as they made their way to the kitchen.

When they reached the kitchen door, Liam's father turned, taking the bat from Liam's hands. He ran through the swinging door, bat raised above his head, screaming like a banshee. Liam was on his dad's heels to watch his back if needed. Fumbling to find the light switch, he flooded the kitchen with light.

Father and son stood in the kitchen, Liam's dad ready to pummel anything that crossed his path, but there was nobody in the kitchen with them. They were alone. The coffee pot had finished brewing and was silent. The only other items out of place were the car keys, which had mysteriously turned up right in the middle of the kitchen table.

"Are those your keys, dad?"

Handing the bat back to Liam and grabbing his keys off the table, his dad turned to the door, yelling, "Everything's okay, Darla. You can come in now."

Liam's mother was waiting on the other side of the kitchen door, cell phone ready with her finger on the phone's "send" button, 9-1-1 already dialed.

"See, Honey, I told you it must be a friendly ghost. It made us coffee, and returned my keys." He swung the keys around his finger.

"Unless it gave the keys back so we could leave, and made the coffee so we would leave *tonight*."

Liam swore he heard the high pitched giggling of a little girl.

Chapter 3

The next morning, Liam's heart started pounding as soon as he walked into the kitchen. The creepiness of last night flooded his mind. He wandered to the sink and looked out the kitchen window, into the backyard searching for his parents. The hair prickled up on the back of his neck as Liam sensed someone standing behind him. He spun around, expecting to see his dad trying to sneak up on him. He was surprised to see nothing; he was alone in the kitchen. He was surprised to find moving into a new house would freak him out this bad. Granted, the house was super creepy, but he was almost in high school, way too old to be acting like a terrified little kid.

He closed his eyes and took a deep breath, hoping when he opened his eyes he would either see one of his parents in the room or would be able to shake the feeling he was being watched. After one breath, he peeked through his squinched up eyelids and found he was still alone, but now he also felt alone.

His stomach rumbled reminding him why he went to the kitchen in the first place; breakfast. As he finished pouring milk into his bowl of Frosted Flakes, a loud knock echoed through the house. He jumped out of his skin, spilling milk all over the floor. He stood frozen to the tile on the kitchen floor, milk dripping off his toes, waiting to see if the pounding would start again.

He heard heavy footfalls of someone coming down the stairs towards the living room and the pounding noise.

"Liam," his father yelled. "The movers are here. Shake a leg!"

Liam released the breath he'd been holding. He was glad no one else was in the kitchen to see him so rattled by a simple knock on the front door. Good thing it wasn't a doorbell, he may have had a heart-attack.

*****

Liam had hoped by filling his new room with all of his old stuff, it would make him feel more comfortable, more at home. While it helped, he couldn't shake the almost constant feeling he was being watched, even followed throughout the large farm house.

After getting his room settled, Liam was ready for a good night's sleep in his own comfortable bed. He slept soundly until exactly 6:47 a.m., when he woke to the sound of someone with a heavy tread thundering up the steps.

Liam sat upright in bed, pulse racing, wondering what the emergency was and waiting for his parents to throw open his bedroom door. As the seconds ticked past and nothing happened, he started to relax.

Then, whoever it was thundered back down the stairs again. Liam waited a few moments longer for something to happen. When nothing did, he lay back down, rolled over on his side, and fell back to sleep. He was going to have to talk to his parents about running up and down the stairs so early.

When Liam made his way downstairs for breakfast, his dad had already left for work. He found his mom humming at the kitchen sink rinsing out her coffee cup.

"What was going on this morning?"

Liam's voice startled his mom who was lost in her own thoughts. Dropping the coffee cup in the sink, she spun around holding a soapy hand to her chest.

"Oh! You scared me. I thought you were still sleeping." She blinked a few times. "I'm sorry, what did you ask me?"

"What happened this morning? I heard someone running up and down the stairs. Did Dad forget something?"

"You heard it too? Your dad didn't, and thought I was losing my mind. It wasn't you?"

Liam cocked his head to the side, "Like I'd be up that early."

"If it wasn't you, then I have no idea what it was," her eyes were wide and Liam noticed her hands trembled.

Looking away from him, the crooked dish towel consumed all of her attention. Straightening the towel for the third time, Liam swore he heard his mom whisper, "I hope we didn't make a mistake moving here."

*****

As Liam was stuffing his mouth full of mashed potatoes at dinner, an ear-splitting slam stopped him in mid-chew.

"What was that," Mom asked.

"Sounded like one of the upstairs doors slamming shut." Dad put his fork down, readjusted his glasses, and pushed back from the table. "I'll go take a look though, just in case. Son, got my back?"

Liam's heart dropped. He didn't want to go investigate upstairs, he wanted to stay right where he was and act like he was just eating his supper. But he knew he should go help his dad, so he swallowed the lump of potatoes in his mouth and pushed back his chair.

"You're not leaving me here by myself." Mom put down her fork. "I'm going too."

When they got to the top of the stairs all of the doors were standing wide open, except for one: the door to his mom's home office. Trailing behind him and Dad, Liam heard Mom make a tiny, whimpering noise when she saw it was her office door which had slammed shut.

Liam's dad pressed his ear to the closed door, listening for any strange sounds coming from inside the room. After a few seconds, he looked back at his family, motioned for them to move back down the hallway and away from the closed office door. He threw the door open, and jumped into the doorway with his arms outstretched and his hands clasped together as if he were holding a gun. Scanning the room, he yelled back over his shoulder, "Clear!"

"I swear, you do watch way too much TV." Mom shook her head, laughing, as she walked into her office and looked around.

"What's that?" She pointed to a large, dark spot on the carpet. "It wasn't here before."

The stain started about a foot away from the wall. It appeared as if someone had spilled an enormous amount of an inky liquid across the wood floor, creating the large, mysterious stain. It was at least two feet in diameter and had rough edges, as if it had been allowed to dry in the irregular pattern and no one had bothered to clean it, before the stain set. The strangest part about the spot was the middle. It looked like a smudged handprint, a small handprint, but a handprint none the less, was smeared in the middle of the large, dark mark.

Mom walked over to the stain and dropped to her knees to get a closer look. She ran her finger along the outline of the stain. "This didn't just happen, it's dry." She looked up at Liam and his dad, her eyes wide again. "I swear I've never seen this before. Have you?"

"I haven't, but then again I wasn't looking for it either," Liam answered, although he was pretty sure he would have noticed it if it had been there.

Darla sighed as she stood up. "I guess I'll see what I can do to clean it up after we finish dinner."

The spot drove Liam's mother crazy. She scrubbed the stain with every cleaning solution, concoction, and home remedy known to man. Each time she cleaned, the stain disappeared, just to come back a few days later. Same place, same size, same smeared handprint in the center. No matter what she tried, the spot returned. In frustration, she tossed a small rug over the stain and placed her small filing cabinet containing all of her research on her ancestors, including her family tree project, on top of the rug. Out of sight, out of mind.

*****

Each morning at 6:47 the forceful footsteps thundering up the stairs continued to wake the family, but after a few days, they had grown used to the noise and were able to fall back to sleep after the footsteps made their descent back down the stairs and then vanished, the house falling silent again.

What they couldn't become accustomed to were the activities surrounding the sun porch. There was almost an unspoken rule in the household: don't spend time alone on the sun porch. It wasn't as if the sun porch was falling apart, it was a bright and beautiful room. It had large windows on every wall, running the length of the porch, including the walls on the sides. The wood floors seemed to help bring the sunlight into the room, absorbing the warmth. It helped that Mom bought furniture which seemed made for this room: big yellow overstuffed chairs, with big yellow overstuffed ottomans to match. The white wicker rocking chairs were so cozy they would envelope Liam's entire body as he sank deep into the pale blue cushions. The porch always seemed to have the sweetest smell too, as if honeysuckles bloomed in vases in every corner of the room. All in all, it seemed to be a comfortable place to spend an afternoon reading a good book or napping; except for the strange, suffocating sensation felt by everyone immediately after they entered the room. In here it wasn't just the feeling of being watched, but the feeling of being stalked.

The doors of the sun porch seemed to open and close by themselves. If someone left the door open, when they returned the door would be closed. At first, Liam was blamed for playing practical jokes and always leaving the door in the opposite way he found it, until the day his mom walked past the sun porch just as the door closed with an audible click, and Liam was outside investigating the old, abandoned barn.

But even stranger than the door opening and closing on its own, was Liam's great- grandmother's old wooden music box. Mom had glued the key on the stem years ago so it wouldn't get lost, but it was always a little difficult to wind. Now, it would play by itself without being wound up. One Sunday afternoon, Liam's mother came running out of the house, screaming like a little girl.

She was out of breath when she found Liam and his dad chopping wood, preparing for the colder Georgia winter.

"You are not going to believe what just happened! She just talked to me."

"Who did? Grandma?" Liam asked, thinking his mom had been on the phone with his favorite relative.

"No, the ghost! I went to close the door to the sun porch again. When I grabbed the door knob I heard my music box playing. At first I thought one of you yahoos might be playing a trick on me, so I called your names and asked if anyone was on the porch. Then I heard it, plain as day." Mom stopped for dramatic effect.

"What?" Liam's pulse quickened. "What did you hear?"

"Momma," his mom replied. "Then I screamed, slammed the door, and ran out of the house. Not one of my finer moments."

"No, but I hope it sets your mind at ease some," her husband replied. "Now we know our ghostie is a little girl looking for her mom, not some psycho, deranged killer."

"True. But now it's kinda sad. If the ghost is a little girl, it means a child died here."

Chapter 4

Before Liam knew it, summer vacation was coming to a screeching halt and it was time to start school. Liam moped around each room as if he were trying to memorize each and every detail before having to go back into the classroom.

"What is wrong with you?" Mom asked one morning between sips of coffee. "You look like you've lost your best friend."

Liam sighed. "Starting school each year is bad enough on its own, but this year it's worse. I don't know any of the kids or the teachers."

"I thought you might be a bit worried about starting a new school, so I called them to see if we could take a little tour before classes start."

"You did what? I don't want to go to school before I have too. I'm still on summer vacation."

"I know, but I thought it might set your mind at ease a bit to see the school to at least know where you're going on the first day. This way you won't look like a complete newbie."

"By eighth grade I'm sure all the kids here already know each other, so I'll already stick out. But I guess it's not a bad idea to at least see where my classes will be. I'd hate to be the dork who gets lost at school on the first day."

After lunch Liam and his mom rode their bikes over to Sumter County Middle School. When they walked into the quiet front office, there was another kid about Liam's age standing at the counter with his mom. His shaggy dark hair hung in his eyes. Even though the temperatures outside were pushing the upper 90's, he wore jeans with rips in the knees. He was sporting a Vans shirt and shoes - so he either was a skater, like Liam, or a poser who just pretended to skate.

While they were waiting for the school secretary to print out their schedules, the moms started talking. The other boy's name was Braydon and he's also in 8th grade and new to the school. It was obvious both mothers thought these facts should make the boys best friends.

Awkward. But Liam figured one of them had to say something. "So, I guess you just moved here too."

"Sorta. I lived here until about three years ago and then we moved to Atlanta when my mom got remarried. Then she divorced practice husband number two." He glared at his mother. "And here I am back in this little town. What's your story?"

"We just moved from Florida. My dad's a park ranger at Andersonville."

"I went there on a field trip years ago; it probably hasn't changed a bit. Same old prison. Same weird vibe. Not much changes around here. Since your dad works out there, have you been over to the old prison grounds yet? The tunnels are wild. I couldn't imagine crawling underground. It's just too creepy."

"Naw, I haven't made it out there yet. I've been too busy helping my mom unpack to go anywhere but here." It was Liam's turn to give his mom a look.

"I know what you mean; I'm actually looking forward to starting school just so I can stop moving furniture."

The secretary returned holding copies of the boys' schedules. It appeared the only class they would have together was Language Arts. After the tour of the school, Liam was glad they'd gone. He knew where he was going, and now he knew at least one person.

*****

When school started, Liam realized he didn't need to worry about making friends. There wasn't any time. Between his grades from his last school and the recommendation of his mother, Liam was enrolled in all advanced classes. His mom always thought he was smarter than he did. He hated all the extra work, but in two of his classes was the cutest girl he had ever met: Ellie.

When he first saw her walking down the hall, surrounded by a group of girls, he felt as if he had been punched in the chest and had the breath knocked out of him. She was gorgeous. She had long blonde hair tied back into a wild, curly ponytail, but some of her curls seemed to escape. Her eyes were big, blue, and beautiful, perfectly framed by the longest eyelashes he had ever seen. Liam wondered if her eyelashes hit her sunglasses. Rounding out her perfect face were her tiny button nose and pouty lips. Her lips were always moving since she always seemed to be chewing on a piece gum. Smacking away and blowing bubbles. Perfect bubbles.

Liam thought whenever he saw her he must have looked like one of those old cartoon characters his parents still sometimes watched; the wolf with his tongue rolling out to the ground, his eyes popping out from their sockets, and little hearts fluttering around his face. He tried to shake the feeling off every time he saw Ellie so she wouldn't think he was a freak.

Language Arts and Social Studies were by far his favorite classes. Everywhere else he felt as if he were getting buried under mountains of growing piles of work. It seemed like once he completed one assignment, his teachers gave him two more.

By the beginning of October, Liam congratulated himself. He was finally getting a handle on all of his school work, so, of course, he received another assignment. This time in one of his favorite classes – Language Arts.

"Okay, class," his teacher said, as the bell rang. "Since it's October, it's time to start thinking about Halloween and creepy Halloween stories. Let's brainstorm. What topics make a great, spooky Halloween story?"

"Witches," one student said.

"Ghosts," another added.

"Excellent," his teacher said. "Any other ideas? Liam?"

"Uh, haunted houses?"

"Good! Now, don't forget we live in a historical area. There were several Civil War skirmishes fought in this part of Georgia, in addition to the old prison for Union soldiers down the road in Andersonville. So don't limit yourselves to typical or traditional Halloween stories. Think outside the box and see what you can come up with."

The class murmured, sharing ideas.

"Alright. Since this is your first big writing assignment of the year, you'll be working with a partner."

The students started shifting their seats around and making eye contact with their friends, reserving their partners.

"Now don't get too excited. I'm picking your partners for you this time."

The students groaned, wanting to choose their own partners.

"As soon as I call your names, get together, and start brainstorming. Do not start your rough draft now. Just jot down ideas today. You'll have plenty of time to start writing later. Any questions?"

No one raised their hand.

"Alright. Ellie and Ashleigh, Liam and Braydon..."

His teacher's voice was drowned out by the shuffling of student's feet and scraping of chairs, as everyone started moving around to sit with their partner.

As soon as Liam gathered up all of his stuff and moved over to Braydon's desk, a loud beep came over the intercom.

"Can you send Braydon to the front office to check out please?"

Typical. He had enough homework the way it was, he couldn't afford to lose a whole class period on this latest project without Braydon. Maybe he could join up with another group today. Maybe Ellie's.

"Sorry, man." Braydon stuffed everything into his backpack. "Dentist appointment. How about we get together this weekend and work on it?"

"Sounds good. We'll start on it then."

*****

The nights were turning cooler as summer led into fall and the Turners were unpacked and settling into their new house. Liam loved the cooler nights. They signaled the start of one of his favorite activities since he was old enough to doodle: writing messages in the fog on the bathroom mirror. He would write simple, one word messages or draw smiley faces and stick figures in the fog. The mirrors in the fall and winter were so much better than when the weather was warmer, simply because in the fall, the mirrors were colder and the showers were much hotter, creating thicker steam and thicker fog. Much better for writing in.

One evening, as Liam was drying off after his shower, he wrapped the towel around his waist and stood before the bathroom sink. Written in the fog were two words: *Hello, Liam.*

"Mom! Dad!" Liam yelled, as he ran out of the bathroom and down the stairs, sliding halfway down in his panic to reach the bottom. "She was in the bathroom while I was taking my shower! She might have seen me naked, too."

"Who was in the bathroom, son?" his dad met Liam outside of the kitchen, drying his hands on a dish towel.

"The ghost! She wrote on the bathroom mirror while I was in the shower."

"What did she write?" His mom asked, her voice a mixture of curiosity and concern.

"Hello, Liam." Liam answered, using a falsetto female voice.

"Did she use that voice?" His dad started laughing, "It would have scared me, too!"

"Stop it, John. Can't you see he's shaken up? I guess I'll have to be the one to be an adult and go upstairs and check it out myself, since you can't take anything seriously."

"Oh, I can be serious." Dad pushed his glasses up on his nose, squinched his eyes and tightened his lips. "How's this?"

His dad's "serious face" would have made Liam laugh if he hadn't been so scared by the message in the mirror.

By the time Liam and his parents made it back upstairs and into the bathroom, the room had cooled enough where the fog had cleared up. The message was gone.

Chapter 5

Saturday morning Braydon skated over to Liam's house, backpack in hand, and ready to get to work.

"Alright I'm here, let's do this," Braydon said. "Where do we start? Do you know anything about writing spooky stories?"

"Sorta. I grew up in St. Augustine, Florida. Since it's the oldest city in the country, we had tons of ghost stories down there. My mom gave tours and I loved to go on them with her at night. Sometimes I would jump tours and listen to another storyteller. There was this one guide who dressed up like a pirate, and had a real hook for a hand. He lost his left hand when he was attacked by a crocodile. He was really cool. Anyway, he told us about an experience at his house one night. It creeped me out so bad, I couldn't sleep for a week. Let me see if I can tell the story like he did."

Liam sat up taller, getting himself into character.

"Gamble Rogers was a local folk singer who became a hero the day he died by saving a man from drowning at the beach. After he died, his daughter had a garage sale at his old house. I knew her, so we got to talking."

"Wait a minute. You knew his daughter?"

"No, you doof. I'm telling the story like I'm the ghost tour guide."

"Oh, okay. Whatever."

Liam shot him a dirty look. "Where was I? Oh, yeah. Talking with Gamble's daughter at the garage sale. Anyway, the conversation came around I was a ghost tour guide.

"Aww, come on. Jump to the good part."

"Patience, my friend. Let the suspense build and quit interrupting."

Liam shook himself back into the storyteller mode.

"Gamble's daughter told me her dad haunts her house. She and her sisters often saw Gamble's image standing in the doorway when they were in the kitchen. Just standing there and watching them. She had my complete attention now.

"We kept talking while I looked around her garage sale. A white rocking chair caught my eye. Gamble's daughter told me it was her dad's favorite rocking chair.

Being an antique dealer, and with the history of the chair belonging to Gamble Rogers, I couldn't pass it up.

"So, I bought the chair and put it out on my front porch. Nothing happened for weeks. One night, I brought my own daughter out on the ghost tour with me. She had an EMF gauge with her. Those are handheld devices used to show any kind of electromagnetic fields around an object. If there's any energy present, it lights up. The more bulbs that light up, the more energy an item has. Anyway, while I was giving my tour, my daughter was running all over the streets of St. Augustine, checking the electromagnetic fields on different objects, in different parts of town. When we got home, for fun, she tested the energy field on the rocking chair: every light lit up! The chair wasn't rocking or moving a bit. Everything else on the porch appeared normal, but there was strong energy coming off of the rocking chair."

"Here's where it's going to get scary, right?"

Liam shot Braydon another look for interrupting and continued without breaking character.

"A few nights later, my girlfriend was over and we were watching a movie. As we sat on the couch, the front door started to open. It opened just wide enough for a person to walk through. We didn't see anything. The door stayed in the same spot for almost a minute; not opening anymore, but not closing either. Trying to be funny, I said, "Well, don't just stand there. Come in and close the door."

"The door creaked closed, as if someone had come in the house and was pulling it closed behind them. It didn't slam shut, like a gust of wind caught it at that precise second, but closed little but little until you heard the CLICK of the lock catch. I got all excited, forgetting everything, including my girlfriend sitting beside me. I had an actual ghost in my living room. Maybe. I needed another sign. I wanted to make sure there actually was a ghost in my house.

"So I asked, "If you're here, give me another sign." Right then I felt a sharp pain in my arm. I looked down to see if something ghostly gripped my arm. No such luck. It was my girlfriend. She had punched me - hard! Her eyes were as big as saucers; you could almost feel the fear radiating from her like a heat lamp.

"What are you doing," she said, "asking for another sign? Something coming in your house wasn't a good enough sign for you? You are going to wake up in the middle of the night with something standing over you, staring down at you. Are you out of your ever lovin' mind?"

"Nothing else happened that night or any night afterwards. A few weeks later I sold Gamble's rocking chair to a local historian, who was also a ghost tour guide and a friend of Gamble's. I'm not sure if Gamble's spirit went with his chair or is still at my house, too scared of getting punched by my girlfriend to make his presence known!"

"It wasn't creepy. You lost sleep over that one? Really?" Braydon rubbed his arms.

"I guess you had to be there," Liam tilted his head, shrugging.

"You know your house is supposed to be haunted, don't you? They say the girl who lived here over a hundred years ago haunts it. She was about our age when she snapped and hacked up her entire family with an axe."

A loud THUMP outside the bedroom door startled the boys. Their eyes widened. Liam tiptoed to the door, opened it, and peeked outside. When he didn't see anything, he closed the door. "You're talking about Lizzy Borden," Liam said. "She didn't live anywhere near here. She lived up in Massachusetts."

"No, I know who Lizzy Borden is, and I'm not talking about her." He pushed his dark bangs out of his eyes. "I'm talking about the girl who murdered her family in this house. Her name was Sarah. Sarah Whitney."

The boys heard another loud THUMP outside the bedroom door. They stopped talking and looked at each other like animals caught in headlights. Liam didn't get up and check this one. "It's just...you know...an old house noise," Liam said.

A crow cawed in the distance.

"Yeah. I'm sure that's it. Anyway," Braydon continued, obviously enjoying his turn at storytelling, "the town was small back then and the church's minister was a little worried when the Whitney family didn't come for church services on Sunday, since everyone in town went to church every Sunday back then. So he came out to the house to check on the family, to make sure no one was sick or anything. When he walked up all the dogs were howling like crazy. He knocked on the door, but no one answered. So he opened the door and walked into the silent house. In every room, he found a family member's bloody, hacked-up remains. He ran out the front door, gagging, and probably peed his pants. What if the murderer was still around? Then he saw Sarah standing on the front porch – alive but covered in blood. The family's dogs surrounded her, still howling, like they were trying to point out the murderer."

The temperature dropped in Liam's bedroom. His shoulders tightened as a shiver ran down his spine.

"What happened to her?" Liam whispered. Off in the distance, the boys heard dogs howling.

"I'm not sure. I think she disappeared or something. You know Mr. Langford, the history teacher, I bet he knows. He finds that kinda stuff interesting."

"Since I live here, I guess I do too."

The boys heard a loud, insistent tapping at the window. Liam's heart dropped to his stomach while he jumped in his own skin. He and Braydon spun around to see what was trying to get in through the bedroom window.

Peering through the glass, the blue gray eye of a crow looked back at them before tapping on the window with his beak.

Chapter 6

Liam bolted upright in bed. Something startled him and woke him from a vivid dream, in which he was passionately kissing Ellie. His heart was pounding, either from the dream or the sudden shock of being awake. He held his breath, listening for whatever it was that woke him up. He strained to see in the pitch black room. He didn't see or hear anything, but the air in his room felt different. It was charged with electricity and very, very cold. The skin along his neck tightened, rippling all the way up through the top of his skull. His entire body started shaking under the thin sheet on the bed.

"Hello? I'm not alone in here, am I?" Liam whispered.

The seconds ticked by like hours as Liam waited for some sort of response.

Finally, a little girl's voice answered, giggling. "No, you're not."

Liam's heart beat against his ribs. Even though his bedroom was freezing, sweat dripped down his face. "Are you Sarah Whitney?" Liam realized he was holding his breath, waiting for an answer.

Footsteps approached his bed.

"No," the voice screamed. "I'm Sarah *Mathis*. I was born a *Mathi*s and I died a *Mathis*. I never took that low down scoundrel Whitney's last name. He was my step-father, not my father."

Liam closed his eyes, his hands trembled, making the sheet move. What was happening? One second she was giggling, the next screaming. He didn't know what to do, so he didn't do anything. The sweet smell of honeysuckle made his head swim.

Liam's palms tingled; he thought he might pass out. His mouth was dry, he swallowed hard. "Why are you here?" His voice cracked, coming out high pitched as if he had sucked all the helium from a balloon.

"I heard you today," Sarah said, much calmer now. "I heard you telling your stories. I need you to help me."

"Help you? How?"

Sarah paused so long, Liam thought he was alone again until he heard her whisper of a sigh. Hearing her uncertainty gave Liam a jolt of more courage. If he didn't help her, who would?

"How do you think I can help you?"

"I didn't do it," Sarah rushed, needing to get the words out now that she started speaking. "I didn't kill my family. Please, I need you to help me find out who did. I need to know who took my family away from me." Her high pitched little girl voice sounded whiney.

Liam thought for a minute. He rubbed his hands across his face, trying to think clearer. "I don't know. This is insane."

"I'm *not* insane!" Sarah wailed.

Liam didn't want her to start screaming again. "Okay, okay. I never said you were."

Liam rubbed the spot about his nose which always crinkled when he thought. He wished he had more time to think about it and make a decision, but didn't think from his brief time with Sarah she would be the kind of ghost who could be put off. She'd probably make his life a nightmare if he told her no.

He filled up his cheeks with air and blew it out. "Well, this probably isn't really happening and is just a bad dream anyway, so...." He took in another deep breath and exhaled slowly, buying more time. "Alright. I must be crazy, but I'll see what I can do...."

Something cold brushed Liam's hand, making Liam shiver more under the lightweight sheet. "I knew you were

45

the one sent to help me. I knew it as soon as I heard you telling your ghost stories." Sarah was giggling again. The cold enveloped his left hand. Was she holding his hand? This was getting weirder and weirder.

"Whoa, now. Wait a minute. I'm not sure about being the one sent to help you. My parents decided to move out here; it wasn't my choice at all. We had no idea the house was haunted when we moved." He hesitated, struck by a thought. "Wait a minute; you know you're a ghost?"

"Of course I know I'm a ghost. What else could I be?" Sarah sounded offended. "But I would rather be called a spirit than a ghost. The word, ghost, just sounds silly and make believe, like I should be floating through the house in a bed sheet, rattling chains or some such nonsense."

"Sorry," Liam said. "I didn't mean to hurt your feelings, but I'm new to all of this, and I think I'm dreaming anyway, so my brain's not working too well right now."

"It's quite alright." Sarah's voice calmed again. "You have taken my news remarkably well. Much better than some of the other children who have lived here."

"I've always wanted to live in a haunted house. I thought it would be pretty cool."

Bam! It sounded as if his jar of loose change fell off of his dresser.

"I will NOT be doing any parlor tricks." She was yelling again.

He sat up straighter in bed. "Sorry, sorry, sorry. I didn't mean it like that. I just meant I always thought it would be cool to know someone else was always there with you. I'd never be by myself. I haven't made any friends yet and being an only child can be lonely sometimes. I'd never ask you to do parlor tricks. I don't even know what those are." His entire body was shaking. He wrapped his arms around his chest to ward of the cold. He heard his heartbeat pounding in his ears.

"I must apologize too, then. I'm a bit sensitive when I think someone wants me to do tricks for them. It also takes a great deal of energy to talk as we are now. I must go soon."

"Wait! Before you go, can you tell me a little more about you? Can I see you? It seems strange to be talking to a voice in my room."

"Tonight I have enough energy to either show myself, or talk a little longer. Which would you prefer?"

"I think I'd rather see you, and put a face with the voice. I can wait a little longer for more details."

The foot of Liam's bed turned into a swirling mass of white, glowing fog. As the fog took the shape of a girl, the colors started to darken, and the shadows deepen. From the sound of her voice, Liam thought she would have been much younger, like six or eight. He was surprised to see she appeared to be closer to his age, maybe fourteen or fifteen.

She was petite, much smaller than he was. Her dark blonde hair was tied back in a thick braid so long it hung almost to her waist. Her eyes shone blue, even in the dark bedroom. While they were wide and hopeful, there was a touch of sadness around the corners. Sarah's small nose was upturned at the end, but perfect for her face. She held her mouth in a grim line of determination; she wasn't frowning, but not smiling either. The lines on her sun tanned face alone told Liam her fourteen years of life hadn't been easy. She appeared to be muscular from years of farm work. Her shoulders were broad and tapered to a thin waist; she must have worked hard and eaten little. The shape of her body reminded Liam of the gymnasts he saw when he watched the Summer Olympics on TV since they too were so tiny yet extremely muscular at the same time.

She was dressed in a nightgown that hung to the floor, and covered every inch of her body below her neck. It was hard to tell what color the gown had been originally, it was so faded from years and years of wearing and washing, the small flowered pattern was barely visible. Her fingertips peeked out from under the long sleeves that covered the rest of her hands. Liam could tell the gown was not made to fit Sarah, but rather it was a hand-me-down from an older sister, or even her mother.

Liam saw Sarah for a few short seconds before she faded in front of his eyes. Before she was gone, Liam heard her whisper, "Please help me."

The room became pitch black again, and the chill in the air disappeared as soon as Sarah did. Liam blinked and shook his head before laying his head on his pillow and closed his eyes, wondering if agreeing to help a ghost was a mistake.

Chapter 7

The next morning as Liam shuffled down the main hall of his middle school, he bit his lip, lost in thought. His mind kept jumping around, wondering how in the world he could help Sarah, if she was in fact real and not a dream. The fog in his head also slowed his feet. He realized he was in the middle of the hall when the tardy bell rang. He sprinted the rest of the way to class.

He pulled the door open an inch at a time, slipped through and was in the process of closing the door when he knew he was busted.

"Ah, Mr. Turner," his teacher, Mr. Langford, announced to the class in his typical monotone voice. Looking down his nose so he could see over his glasses, he held Liam's gaze, "I'm so glad you could join us today."

Liam's jaw tightened. Most of the time Mr. Langford was an okay teacher, as far as teachers go, but he despised students coming in late and disrupting his class. If you came in late to his class, there was no hope of slipping by him. You could always expect some kind of public announcement. Liam looked around for Ellie to make sure she hadn't seen his late arrival and heard Mr. Langford's snippy comments, but her face was buried under her waterfall of curls, blowing a bubble with her gum, deep in discussion with the girl behind her so she didn't see or hear a thing.

Liam relaxed and decided to keep his mouth shut. Sometimes students argued with Mr. Langford, to make the vein in the side of his neck pop out and delay the start of class. But Liam remembered how Braydon had said Mr. Langford was also a local history buff. Maybe his teacher could help him with Sarah's mystery. Liam needed to get his teacher on his side rather than pick a fight with him.

Liam muffled a quick "sorry," before he sat quietly, ignoring Mr. Langford's comments.

After a mind numbing lecture on the causes of the Civil War, Liam wondered how to ask Mr. Langford about Sarah's mystery. Like ripping off a Band-Aid, Liam decided to just do it fast. He walked up to Mr. Langford who stood in the hallway, waiting for the next class to enter.

"Sorry for being late today, sir. I didn't sleep well last night and my mind is still hazy."

Mr. Langford rocked back on his heels, crossing his arms over his chest. "While I understand it, Liam, it's still no excuse for being tardy. Once you get in the real world and get a job, your boss isn't going to care if you didn't get any sleep. Your boss will only care if you get to work on time. That's the lesson I'm trying to teach you kids: personal responsibility."

Liam took a deep breath, it wasn't going to be easy asking this teacher for help, but he needed to try.

"Mr. Langford, could I come and talk to you after school today? A friend came over to my house the other day to work on our Halloween writing project. He told me a family was murdered in my house."

"Ahhh, you must live in the old Whitney House." Mr. Langford came alive; his voice had a hint of excitement to it now. "Yes, come by after school today and I'll tell you what I know. Fascinating story, really. They say the daughter, Sarah, killed her entire family."

Students started filing in for class.

"But run along now," Mr. Langford said with a new sparkle in his green eyes. "You don't want to be tardy for your next class, now do you?"

*****

Liam was distracted all day, wondering what information Mr. Langford would share with him. Sarah said she didn't do it, but Liam had the feeling Sarah might not be the most mentally stable person he'd ever met. One minute she was giggling, the next minute she was screaming at him. She seemed to be one strange girl. Make that one strange spirit. He wondered what evidence the town had to accuse her in the first place. It must have been pretty convincing since most everyone still believed she murdered her family over a hundred and fifty years later.

Finally the dismissal bell rang. Liam fought the flood of students leaving school as he made his way back to Mr. Langford's classroom.

"Liam, my boy, have a seat." Mr. Langford removed his glasses, pointing to a chair in front of his large desk. "You were curious about the murders at the Whitney House. It was quite tragic. Poor girl accused of murdering her family in cold blood." Mr. Langford trailed off, shaking his head. "But, like all good stories, one must start at the beginning."

"The Mathis family was fairly well to do before the Civil War broke out. They were cotton farmers, and had a large house, Whitehurst, built right before the war started."

"Is that where Mathisville got its name? The Mathis family?"

Mr. Langford nodded. "It is. They were one of the few families living in the area at the time, so they were able to name the small town whatever they wanted. And since they were the wealthiest family in the area at the time, and one of the few families, Mr. Mathis named the town after himself."

"But why is it called the Whitney house then, instead of the Mathis house?"

"Mr. Mathis died in a peanut farming accident."

"But I thought you said they were cotton farmers."

"They were. Well, mostly." Mr. Langford took off his glasses and started cleaning them with a tissue from his desk. "Mr. Mathis was definitely a man ahead of his time. He had dedicated a couple of acres to peanuts. He was also an inventor of sorts and tried to create a tool to help harvest his peanuts. The records are quite vague, but somehow Mr. Mathis was killed by his own invention."

Mr. Langford pointed his glasses at the fluorescent lights. Peering through them, he must have found them smudge free since he placed them back on the bridge of his nose.

"Widows didn't stay alone and unmarried for long, especially rich ones. Benjamin Whitney swept Molly Mathis off her feet and they were married within a year of her husband's death."

"Wow. She didn't waste much time, did she?"

"It wasn't unusual back then. The war had already broken out, her husband had been killed and her son was away fighting for the Confederacy. She may have felt her family of young women needed the protection of a man. Or maybe she just didn't want to be alone. Who knows? All we know for sure is he took over the family home and it has been called the Whitney House ever since."

Liam squirmed in the hard chair.

"But I digress." Mr. Langford pulled himself back to the story at hand. "Back to Sarah and the murders.

"Sarah was the middle of five children. Her older brother, the only son, died in the Battle of the Wilderness, fighting on the side of the Confederacy. She also had one older sister, and twin younger sisters. Some people wonder if that was the reason why Sarah killed them: the middle child syndrome. She was tired of being forgotten or ignored and just wanted some attention herself. Others think when the family lost everything in the war, like most Southern families, they all sort of mentally snapped – Sarah the hardest."

Mr. Langford shifted his weight, his chair squealing in protest. "Anyway, regardless of the catalyst, the whole family, with the exception of Sarah, was murdered in the middle of the night on June 10, 1865."

"I'm guessing it happened on a Saturday night, since the preacher found the bodies after church on Sunday." Liam leaned forward, interrupting.

"I see you've already been doing some research." A hint of approval was evident in his teacher's voice. "You are correct. While speculation abounds, one thing everyone agrees with is on Sunday the preacher went to the Whitney house and discovered all of the bodies and Sarah, very much alive and covered from head to toe in blood.

"They say Sarah was speechless, either from the horror of seeing her family dead, or the trauma of killing them herself. Since she couldn't tell anyone what happened to her family and since she was covered in their blood, the townspeople assumed she was guilty of committing the vicious crime herself."

"I also heard dogs were surrounding her, howling."

"Right, again. Her family owned several dogs. After the murders if even one of the dogs saw Sarah, all of them would start howling. From what I understand, it was eerie. People back then took signs from nature; they figured the dogs witnessed the murders and were trying to point out Sarah as the killer."

Liam squinched his face, confused. "What happened to her? Was there any kind of trial?"

Mr. Langford leaned his arms on his desk, making his chair creak. "No. She wasn't even arrested. The preacher was terrified by the sight of the mutilated bodies and howling dogs, so he ran back to town, leaving Sarah standing on the porch, still covered in blood. When he came back with the sheriff, Sarah was nowhere to be found."

"So, where was she?"

"While the sheriff was walking through the house, investigating the crime scene, someone yelled that Sarah was hiding in the barn. She jumped onto one of the family horses and galloped out of the barn and past the house. All of this happened before the sheriff could make it out to the porch. A deputy tried to stop her by running out in front of the house in order to head off her horse. It didn't work. The horse spooked instead of stopping. It reared up and flipped over, landing on Sarah."

Sarah's sad eyes popped into Liam's mind. Poor thing didn't stand a chance. Knowing the answer, but needing to hear it anyway, Liam asked, "Was she ok?"

"Oh, no. When the horse got up, Sarah didn't. The fall killed her."

Liam grimaced. "How?"

"It broke her neck. The townspeople didn't care how she died, just that the person who they felt murdered the entire Whitney family was dead. Whether or not she was the actual murderer didn't matter much to them."

"What do you mean? They didn't even try to investigate what happened? I mean, aside from being covered in blood, and not able to talk about it, why do they think she did it? The evidence seems a bit weak."

"Because she tried to run away. Running from the scene of a crime is usually a good indication of guilt."

"Usually. But I get the feeling you don't think Sarah did it?"

Mr. Langford tapped a pencil against the desk, looking up. "The one thing I've never understood is how she could physically hack her family to pieces. I'm not sure if she had the strength. Plus, she was just a child. Even in a rage, I've always found it hard to believe a teenage girl could kill her entire family with an axe. Using one would take a

58

tremendous amount of strength and I just don't know if a fourteen year old girl has that kind of strength or why no one over-powered her and stopped her."

Liam thought back to the angry, muscular girl with broad shoulders who appeared to him the night before. He could picture her swinging an axe with ease in a berserk rage; the girl had a temper. Liam tried to focus on his teacher and not on his own deadly vision of Sarah.

"Mr. Langford, could someone else, maybe a slave or something, have murdered the family?" Liam asked.

"I wondered about it too, but unfortunately not. They released their slaves with everyone else, when Union soldiers emancipated the slaves on the courthouse steps a few weeks earlier. Like I said, the Civil War left the family without much money. The Whitney family didn't have any money to pay hired hands to work the fields, so the family ended up working it themselves. There wasn't anyone on the plantation at the time except for the family. I've always wondered though, if some disgruntled former slave might have snuck back and killed the family."

Liam didn't know what to think. There was no one else but the family around during the time of the murders and if Sarah and the rest of the family had taken to working in the fields, well....He didn't know how much strength it would take to axe a human, but if she could swing a sickle in the field, why not an axe in the house?

Chapter 8

Liam lay awake in bed that night, wondering if Sarah was going to show up. He was torn between wanting to talk to her and wishing she would stay away. He wasn't in the mood to be yelled at when she was in one of her moods. It didn't matter what he wanted. Sarah didn't appear, she didn't talk to him, and the temperature in his bedroom didn't drop.

After lying awake all night waiting for Sarah, it was even more difficult for Liam to drag himself to school than the previous day. He couldn't stop rubbing his eyes and even helped himself to his parent's coffee. Spitting out the bitter black drink, he couldn't see how anyone would ever willingly drink the stuff.

*****

As he walked into Mr. Langford's class, Mr. Langford pulled him aside.

"I've been thinking about your house. Believe it or not, Sumter County had somewhat of a newspaper even back then, *The Sumter County Tribune*. I think it came out weekly. Anyway, the local library should be able to help you find copies of the story. You might want to check that out. The old articles should have some valuable information about the murders."

That was all Liam needed to hear. After school he hopped on his skateboard, and headed to downtown Mathisville. As he skated down the narrow roads, surrounded by ancient oak trees with tendrils of Spanish moss hanging from the branches, he wondered if Sarah walked past the same trees, the same Spanish moss. The thought heightened Liam's senses. What else did he pass every day and take for granted? What places in town were exactly the same now as they were in Sarah's time? Liam skated up to the library, an old building which appeared as if it had been there since the beginning of time, but the cornerstone read 1903, meaning Sarah had never seen it. What a depressing thought. Confusion consumed him: Should he be afraid of Sarah who may have killed her entire family or should he be filled with sadness for Sarah and for the life she was never able to live?

Arriving at the library, Liam pushed the old, heavy wooden doors open. The doors creaked on their ancient hinges. His spine stiffened as he walked inside, his skateboard under one arm.

The librarian's line-wrinkled face made her seem as old as the building and about as warm as the old stone too. She wasn't overly friendly until Liam told her he lived in the Whitney house and was curious about its history. That piqued her interest in finding information and helping him with his research. He left out the part where Sarah asked him for help; he didn't think the librarian would be as eager to help if she knew it were for a ghost.

She led Liam to a dark, musty smelling room holding what looked like an enormous, ancient computer.

"Newspapers as old as what you're looking for are stored on microfilm. This way we can save the history, but also save space for more current writings. This beast," she said as she tapped on the side of the giant machine, "is a microfilm reader. The films are kept over here and are in chronological order."

She flipped through the films.

"This should be the one you want. It covers all of 1865."

She sat down at the massive machine, flipped a switch on the side, and waited as it wheezed to life.

"This thing is so ancient, it might take it a few minutes to warm up. Once it does, I'll show you how to use it and then I need to get back to the circulation desk."

After his short lesson in prehistoric technology, Liam flew through pages of the weekly paper, becoming familiar with life in 1865. Most of the articles contained more gossip than actual news, and Liam caught himself skimming the sensational articles instead of closely reading them. He slowed down when he came to June, reading each page instead of skimming the headlines. It wasn't long before he saw:

SHOCKING CRIME

Whitney Family Hacked To Pieces in Own Home

The community of Sumter County was shocked this morning to hear an atrocious deed had been committed, and the Whitney family had fallen victim to a murderer. The deed was committed in their home, Whitehurst, where Benjamin Whitney lived in happiness with his wife and children.

It is supposed that an axe was the instrument of death, as the bodies of the victims were hacked almost beyond recognition.

Father John Murphy ran into town after going to check on the family following Sunday's service and was heard crying "Murder! Go for the sheriff!"

Officers Toole and Clement were sent to investigate the case. Once in the house, they found a terrible sight. In their bedroom, Benjamin and Molly Whitney presented a sickening vision. Their faces were hacked to pieces and blood covered the bodies and had soaked into their clothing. Everything about the room was in order, and it is presumed they were asleep when the deadly blows were struck, thus giving them no chance to make an outcry.

Further investigation found another dreadful sight. In their beds were daughters Elizabeth, Mary, and Louise dead where they had been struck, each felled by the deadly axe.

Dr. Bowman was the first physician to arrive, but all lives were extinct.

Missing was daughter, Sarah, who according to Father Murphy had been seen alive that morning, apparently unharmed but covered in blood.

After a careful hunt over the premises, Sarah burst from the barn attempting to flee on horseback. It was reported she was caught in fits of hysterics as she was laughing uncontrollably and muttering strange words, their meaning unknown.

Sarah Whitney did not have time to produce an alibi, as she met her death when her fleeing horse reared and fell, killing her on the spot. What her motive was for these fiendish murders is hard to tell, as Mr. Whitney was always kind to her and his other step-children.

After a careful examination of the victims, the conclusion was reached that the wounds were inflicted by a heavy, sharp instrument such as an axe or hatchet. The murder weapon has not been found.

Staring at the grainy letter on the screen, Liam pushed himself back from the microfilm reader, hit the button to print out the article, and rubbed his dry eyes. "Wow," he whispered. "Who knew?"

Chapter 9

Liam woke up freezing. He glanced over at the clock on his nightstand. 2:04. He wondered if he'd ever be able to get a full night's sleep again. He inhaled through his nose. The sweet smell of honeysuckle filled the room. Sarah had to be close. He stretched his arms over his head, trying to wake up, and saw his breath coming out in a smoky stream. Sarah was definitely close.

"Sarah? Are you in here?"

"Yes, Liam," she giggled from somewhere near the foot of the bed. "I am here."

Liam pushed himself up on his elbows, closed his eyes and inhaled deeply.

"Did you find out who murdered my family?"

"Not yet." He didn't want to tell Sarah about the newspaper article, just yet. He needed more information before he shared anything with her.

"I did not do it," Sarah whimpered.

"Why did you run away?"

"I don't know. In hindsight I can see how foolish it was to try to run away, but I was scared. I didn't know what I should do or where I should go. I knew crowds of people were going to show up, but I was not ready to talk to anyone. I had just found my entire family dead."

Liam pulled up his knees and hugged them. "Tell me what happened. I need to know so I can help."

"The night before was sweltering. I was sweating while I lay in bed, it was so hot. Sometime during the night, I snuck out to the porch, opened all of the windows, and laid on the settee on the porch. The breeze cooled me, and I was able to fall asleep.

When I woke the next morning, the sun was already up. I didn't hear any sounds from anyone in the house, so I walked into the kitchen and found it empty. I thought it was strange. Even if I had slept past breakfast, Mother still would have been in there cleaning up or preparing for our noon meal. There was no sign I had missed breakfast: no smell of cooked biscuits and bacon or heat from the fire. The kitchen was empty and cold."

Liam caught a whiff of honeysuckle as a cold breeze brushed his feet, as the window blinds swayed.

"I walked upstairs and peeked in on the twins. As soon as I crossed the threshold to their room, the smell of blood gagged me and I staggered backwards into the hallway. I still had not seen them yet, but smelled the strong odor of blood. I peered in the room and saw the blood-stained sheets. I turned and ran to Elizabeth's room.

"I saw poor Elizabeth in her bed. Her face was smashed in, but I knew it was her. She had the prettiest blonde hair out of all of us girls; I would recognize her hair anywhere. I stepped out and retched in the hallway."

Liam's change jar jingled on his dresser. He imagined Sarah sliding different coins back and forth across the surface as she told her story.

"I was afraid to go to Mother and Mr. Whitney's room; I didn't want to see if they suffered the same fate. But I knew I must. The door to their bedroom was ajar. When I looked in, I saw both of them on the floor. They were lying in such unnatural poses. Even though I couldn't see their faces through all of the blood-matted hair, I knew without a doubt it was Mother and Mr. Whitney."

At the mention of her step-father, Liam thought he caught a flash of Sarah's outline standing by the foot of his bed. It was gone as quickly as it had happened.

"I ran out of the house, screaming until I reached the yard."

"How did you get blood all over you?"

"As I sat crying on the porch, I realized I had not actually seen Mary or Louise. Maybe one of them had survived the massacre. So, I went back into their room to check on the twins. Mary was still in bed, but Louise was not. I found her lying on the floor, wedged between the bed and the wall."

Sarah's voice caught, as if she were remembering the sight of her sister, lying dead on the floor. She was quiet for a few seconds.

"I'm unsure whether she was trying to get away and was attacked once she was out of bed, or if the force of the attack knocked her out of bed. Either way, I couldn't just leave her lying on the floor like a piece of rubbish. So I picked her up and placed her back in her bed, next to Mary."

"Did you run for help?"

"No. To be honest, the thought hadn't occurred to me. Living far from town, our closest neighbor was miles away. We were almost completely self-sufficient out here. We had to be.

"I was devastated. My family was dead. I couldn't move off of the porch. I heard the animals start to complain since they hadn't been fed yet and were hungry. But I just couldn't make myself move."

Again, Sarah paused. Liam thought she was finished talking before he heard a deep sigh.

"By the time Father Murphy came, it must have been close to noon. The animals still hadn't been fed. All of them were complaining loudly by then. The dogs were baying from the yard, trying to get me to feed them. I had stopped crying, but still couldn't get my feet to move.

"Father Murphy didn't see me when he entered the house, only after he ran out of our house. I must have given him quite a fright, being covered in blood and with the dogs howling, after the gruesome sight he had just witnessed. He didn't try to speak. Just took one look at me and he ran toward town.

Seeing him run off startled me. The spell was broken and I was able to move again. I knew I needed to feed the animals, if for no other reason than to quiet them down. While feeding them, I realized I didn't want to be anywhere near the house anymore. The reason I was still alive was because I slept on the porch the night before. Had I been in my room like the rest of the family, I'm sure I would have met the same fate. Maybe the person who murdered my family was still nearby."

Liam hadn't considered the murderer might still be lurking around the house after killing the family, waiting for a chance to kill Sarah too. A dark shadow moved towards the bed. There was slight pressure, as if Sarah had sat next to him to continue her story.

"I went to the barn, planning to flee. By the time I had one of the horses tacked up, there were swarms of people milling around. I didn't know if I would be able to talk yet, without bursting into tears, so I tried to leave. One of the sheriff's deputies startled my horse and he reared back. I tumbled off and felt a sharp pain in the back of my head. I don't know anything after that."

"Was anyone else around during that time, like slaves or random travelers? Anyone out of the ordinary?" Liam asked.

The pressure on the bed moved. Sarah must have stood up.

"No, we didn't have any more slaves. There was no one at Whitehurst but our family."

"Was anyone upset with your family; maybe they came back for revenge for something?"

"Some may have had issues against my step-father. He was a mean and vile man. But not against Mother, Elizabeth, or the twins. No one could have a disagreement against them. They never mistreated or cheated anyone." Sarah sniffed. "I must go now."

"Wait! I have some more questions."

But before Liam could ask them the temperature in his room returned to normal. He knew he was alone again.

Chapter 10

Liam's heart was pounding when he woke up. He glanced over at the clock on his nightstand. He had overslept. Either he had become so accustomed to hearing those footsteps tearing up and down the stairs he was subconsciously ignoring them, or the footsteps had stopped. He sat thinking about it when he realized he hadn't heard the footsteps running up and down the stairs since Sarah asked for help. Maybe now that she had his attention, she'd stopped her early morning runs.

Liam couldn't afford to think about it or he'd be late for school. He'd been getting in trouble these last few days for being so distracted; he didn't need a tardy on top of everything.

Grabbing a banana for breakfast as he ran through the kitchen, he heard his parents talking.

"It's finally gone. I'm not sure what it was that did the trick, but it's gone now," his mom said.

"Either you found something that permanently removes stains, or our little ghostie has accepted us and is tired of driving you crazy," Dad chuckled.

Liam stopped in his tracks. "What's gone?"

"Oh, you remember the stain that was on the floor of my office? The one that looked like an old blood stain with the smeared handprint? I finally scrubbed it out. I cleaned it again days ago, and it hasn't come back yet."

Liam remembered he hadn't heard Sarah's footsteps in a few days, and now the stain on the floor had disappeared. Maybe he was right: now that Sarah had his attention, she was a little more at peace and could stop running up and down the stairs every morning.

*****

When Liam walked into history class Mr. Langford pulled him back out into the hallway. "Liam, did you find anything at the library?"

"I did. I found an article about the murders and Sarah's death. But it took me so long to figure out how to use the microfilm projector I ran out of time. I'm going back after school to see if I can find anymore articles."

"I'd be interested in reading anything you find. I've always found the case fascinating – being a local murder and all."

"Sure thing, Mr. Langford," Liam said as he entered the room, making his way back to his desk.

Liam's mind kept wandering back to the article he'd found and Sarah's story. How would he feel if he woke up and found his parents dead? Would he have reacted the same way she did or would he have thought to call for help? Would he have snapped and laughed uncontrollably too? What if he were accused of murdering his parents? Would he run away or stay and try to clear his name? Too many questions he'd hopefully never have to answer.

After school he skated down the oak tree lined streets to the library. There was a different librarian behind the desk; Liam knew he'd have to explain his life story all over again before he could get in the microfilm room. Thankfully this librarian didn't seem to care one way or the other about what Liam was doing as long as he didn't have to get up and help.

"Got it." Liam said, as he headed back into the dark, musty room which held the giant wheezing microfilm reader.

Settling back with the one hundred and fifty year old headlines, in the hardest chair he had ever sat in, Liam spent the rest of the afternoon reading about the past. His heart just about stopped when he saw the headline:

A Sad Accident

We regret to learn of the death of **Robert Townsend Mathis**, of Mathisville, from a very tragic accident on February 4, 1863.

The deceased was engaged with his latest farming implement at Whitehurst when he became entrapped in one of the wheels. Before the contraption could be stopped the flesh of his leg was removed from his hip to his ankle. He had expired on the spot before assistance could be rendered.

The deceased was born in Atlanta Georgia in 1810; married Mary Elizabeth Pritchard, whom he affectionately called Molly, and moved south in 1848, establishing Mathisville. He engaged chiefly in growing cotton and was a pioneer on the forefront of peanut farming.

Robert Mathis leaves behind numerous family members to mourn his loss, with whom we are sure many will sympathize.

Liam blew his hair of out his eyes. What a gruesome and painful way to die. He wondered who found the body; if it were Sarah herself or another member of the family. He couldn't believe how much tragedy one family could endure. Life sure was difficult and dangerous back then. Scrolling a little further, the Mathis name popped up again.

MATHIS, JONATHAN – 59th Calvary Regiment, Co G

Virginia, May 6, 1864. Whereas, we have received intelligence of the death of Jo. Mathis. In his death the company has lost a brave and honorable fellow soldier and friend. He endeared himself to us all with his manly conduct. Such soldiers are not to be found every day, and the loss of one such as he, is deeply felt. We tender to his parents and other relations our sympathies on this mournful occasion.

It wasn't until the librarian turned off the lights that Liam realized it was time to go. He looked at his watch. He had spent the last three hours poring over the old microfilms and had not found another word about Sarah or her family aside from the obituaries. It appeared Mr. Langford was right, the townspeople accused Sarah based on the evidence of her being the sole survivor and covered with blood, and since she died trying to flee, it confirmed her guilt. Once she died, the crime was considered solved, with no need to investigate any further, no need to waste any more newsprint on the story. Except for the fact Sarah said she didn't kill her family. If she was telling the truth, the murderer got off scot-free for their fiendish crime.

*****

A few nights later, Liam was working on his part of the ghost story for writing class, when he shivered. What he was writing wasn't terrifying, so it must have been the temperature drop in his room. He tested his theory by exhaling sharply, and sure enough, his breath came out in a smoky stream. His pulse sped up and his heart started pounding.

"Sarah?"

"Yes. I am here. Did you find out who killed my family?"

"Not yet. It seems once you died there was no reason to look for the killer since they thought you did it. I kinda hit a dead end with it." Liam cringed at his poor choice of words.

"I thought of something," she said, apparently not noticing Liam's word choice. "During the summer, the Union soldiers were released from Camp Sumter. Some of them stopped by the farmhouse, offering to work in exchange for a meal or a place to spend the night. Mother was always kind to them, upset with the poor treatment they received while in prison, and couldn't turn anyone away, much to Mr. Whitney's displeasure. Most stayed for a day or two; but there was this one man, Mr. Greenly, he stayed for a few days before he disappeared, without a word of thanks for our hospitality I might add. He snuck out – a thief in the night. After all we'd done for him, he had the nerve to steal mother's new wooden music box and one of our horses."

"But what about the other soldiers you mentioned? They might have come back too. Do you remember their names?"

"They weren't with us as long as Mr. Greenly, nor did they leave surrounded by dramatic circumstances as he did."

Chapter 11

Lightning flashed across Liam's eyelids. Thunder rattled the windows and shook the house. He glanced at his clock radio. It was dark. The power was out. His heart pounded. While he loved rainy days, he couldn't stand thunderstorms. The lightning flashed again and made everything in the room seemed unreal, flickering supernaturally in the light. Thunder boomed, and he could feel the vibrations in his teeth. He tightened his jaw.

He caught a glimpse of Sarah standing at the foot of his bed with an axe. The image was gone and the room became black again.

"Sarah?"

No response. Liam exhaled sharply, seeing if his breath was foggy. Nothing.

Again, lightning lit the room. There wasn't anything at the foot of his bed. Liam laid his head back against his pillow. His eyes must be playing tricks on him. He decided it would be best if he just kept them closed, even if he couldn't sleep.

His mind kept returning to the name Sarah had mentioned. Nat Greenly. It sounded so familiar, but he just couldn't place it. Maybe there was mention of it in the old newspaper articles. The name danced on the edge of Liam's foggy mind, close enough to torment him, but not clear enough to give him any information. Still struggling to make sense of the name, Liam fell back into a fitful, dreamless sleep.

*****

Liam found himself looking forward to Mr. Langford's history class. Not the class itself, but talking to Mr. Langford about Nat Greenly, and asking him how to find out information about the mystery man.

Liam toted all of his books around with him so he could skip going to his locker before class, and avoid being late. "Mr. Langford," Liam said, out of breath from running to class with his heavy backpack. "How do I find out about a soldier from Camp Sumter?"

"Camp Sumter? I haven't heard it called that in a long time; most people around here just call it Andersonville.

What's the name of the soldier? Is he one of the more famous ones?"

"I'm not sure. His name is Greenly."

"Greenly…Greenly…Hmm. He's not one of the famous soldiers, at least I've never heard of him. Where did you get his name?"

Liam had to think fast and make up something; he knew his teacher wouldn't believe a word he had to say if he said he talked to a ghost. "Yesterday, when I went back to the library, I saw mention of his name. He passed through town around the time of the murders. I just thought…"

"…a bitter Union soldier killing a poor, unsuspecting southern family?"

"Something like that." Liam chewed the inside of his lip.

"Let me think on it. I know of a student who might be able to help you. She's from a family of police investigators and journalists, so she is quite good with research. I'll talk to her today. Come back after school and I'll let you know what she says."

*****

After school, Liam rushed back to Mr. Langford's class, fighting against the rush of students heading out the doors, like a salmon swimming upstream.

"You didn't waste much time getting back. I talked with Ellie about your project..."

"Ellie McDonald? The Ellie who's in my class?"

"Yes, the Ellie who's in your class. Anyway, she agreed to help you conduct some research in exchange for some extra credit. Here's her number. I told her you'd call soon. If you hurry, you can still catch your bus."

"Thanks, Mr. Langford," Liam said as he rushed out the door, crushing Ellie's phone number in his hand. It had started raining again, and after being up half the night listening to the thunder, he was tired and didn't want to spend the next hour walking home in the rain and risk her number being washed away. He stood in shock as his bus pulled away from the curb, leaving him behind.

"Err," Liam growled, but figured instead of walking the entire way home, he'd stop by the library and check out the microfilms for any mention of Greenly's name. What a day to leave his skateboard at home.

By the time he walked the few short blocks to the library, his clothes were sticking to his skin from the rain, but thankfully Ellie's number was mostly dry in his hand.

He waved to the librarian as he walked back to the microfilm room. He was a pro with the ancient equipment now, and didn't need to stop for assistance. He grabbed the film containing the year 1865, turned on the microfilm reader, eased into the chair, and fell back into the past.

Liam's eyes felt gritty after skimming the articles for Greenly's name for what felt like hours. No luck. Not a word about the former Union soldier. Tying to ignore the jitters in his gut about calling her, he hoped Ellie would have some better ideas for research. He'd reached a dead end by himself with the old newspaper articles. He needed help.

The rain had stopped by the time Liam stepped out onto the stone steps of the library. At least he didn't have to dodge raindrops walking home, just puddles.

After dinner, and fighting the lima beans that threatened to come back up, Liam picked up the phone. His fingers shook as he dialed the number Mr. Langford had given him.

"Hello?"

"May I speak with Ellie, please?"

"Speaking."

"Hi. My name is Liam? I'm in your Language Arts and Social Studies class?" Liam cringed, he sounded so stupid.

Nothing to do now but tell her why he called. "Mr. Langford gave me your number. He said you were willing to help me with a project."

"That's right." He heard her gum snap.

Liam closed his eyes. He could picture her long, blonde ringlets bouncing with each smack. Maybe she was even biting her bottom lip like she did whenever she was thinking.

"Mr. Langford said you were trying to find out information on a soldier who was kept at Andersonville. Have you gone out there to look through their records?"

"Uh, no. I didn't really know where to start."

"Okay. Have you Googled the soldier's name?"

"Uh, no on that too."

Ellie sighed.

Liam scrambled to explain. "Being out here, they don't offer Internet in our area. I'm kinda stuck in the dark ages."

"Well, I recommend we take a trip to the prison to look through whatever records they have on their soldiers. Do you have any plans this weekend?"

"Um, I don't think so."

"Good. It's not too far to bike to. Let's meet on Saturday around ten-ish. You can tell me all about your project when we get there. Oh, and bring money for lunch, we might be there awhile."

"Got it. I'll see you at ten."

Liam heard a click as Ellie hung up without saying another word.

"She thinks I'm an idiot."

Chapter 12

Liam didn't want to keep Ellie waiting, so he skated up to the Andersonville Visitors Center at 9:45 on Saturday morning. She pedaled into the parking lot driveway at 9:50 and headed over to Liam.

"Hi," the words got caught in Liam's throat and came out a little squeaky. He tried to cover it with a cough, but didn't think he pulled it off well.

"*Now* I know who you are. I was trying to put a face with your name and couldn't do it. I'll always remember you as my Social Studies savior. Mr. Extra Credit."

Liam felt his face grow hot. How in the world was he going to be able to keep his cool around her all day?

While Ellie locked up her bike, Liam started to tell her what he knew about the Whitney murders, and in particular, Mr.Greenly.

"Why are you researching this?" She asked, cutting him off. "I mean, aside from living in the old Whitney house, what's the interest?"

Thinking quick and saying something he thought Ellie would accept he said, "I mean, I obviously want to know what happened in my house, but Mr. Langford's giving me extra credit for his class too."

"Oh, gotcha."

"Any idea where to start the search?"

"My mom's a journalist and she always says to start with the easiest and the most obvious. I figure we should start with the park rangers at Andersonville and see where it leads us."

Liam was glad he'd caught a break. His dad wasn't working today. Liam wanted to talk to someone who had been there awhile and might know about Greenly. Plus he didn't want his dad embarrassing him in front of Ellie.

He followed her to the double doors and walked into the building.

A bell tinkled. The ranger at the desk looked up, her old sun-leathered face breaking into a smile.

"Hi. Welcome to Camp Sumter. Feel free to look around. If you have any questions, let me know. We have a short film on the history of the prison starting at eleven if you're interested. "

"Actually," Liam said, "is there any way of finding out information about an individual soldier who was kept here as a prisoner?"

"Possibly. Which prisoner are you interested in?"

"Greenly."

"Do you have a first name? You might get swamped with just a last name.

"That's all I have though," Liam said.

"Alright, then. Let me check his name in the cemetery database and see what we get."

"No, he didn't die here." Liam shook his head. "I know he made it out alive. But that's all I know. I'm not sure where he came from, or where he went after he left here."

"Just a name is not a lot to go on, but I'll try and see what I can come up with."

A family with five screaming kids ran into the museum.

"Tell you what," the ranger said, raising her voice to be heard over the yelling children, "leave the soldier's name with me, and you two take a tour of the grounds. Since it's Saturday, we have a guided ranger tour. When I have a minute, I'll run the name. Stop back and I'll let you know what I come up with. Sound good?"

Liam nodded. "We'll see you in a bit."

"Whew!" Ellie said, fingering an escaped hair curl, as they headed toward the main door. "It was getting pretty loud in there. I'm ready to head outside."

Liam grunted in agreement. "Where do you think we should start?" he asked, ready to change the subject.

"While you were talking to the ranger, I grabbed a map and thumbed through one of the guide books. According to the book, all the prisoners entered through the North Gate. I think we should start too, where the prisoners did."

Liam and Ellie entered the prisoner area, just as a ranger was getting ready to start his next presentation.

"Great. Let's join this group and see what life was like for these guys," Liam suggested.

"Sure beats wandering around aimlessly."

"Good afternoon," the ranger began, adjusting his hat to shield his eyes from the bright Georgia sun. "Welcome to Camp Sumter, or Andersonville, as it's more commonly called today." The ranger's southern accent was so thick, Sumter came out as "Sumptah." Trying not to be distracted by the ranger's accent, Liam focused harder on the presentation.

"During the two years it was used as a prisoner of war camp for Union soldiers, it housed over 45,000 soldiers.

The most soldiers this twenty-six acre piece of land held at any one time was just over 33,000."

Liam looked over the small piece of land and had a difficult time imagining 3,000 adults here, much less 33,000. Between the heat and the filth, it must have smelled awful with all of those sweaty, dirty bodies. Looking around him now, almost everyone on the tour had paper fans from the gift shop to cool themselves somewhat. The poor prisoners didn't even have that luxury.

The ranger walked backwards, leading the group of hot, sweaty tourists. "Unfortunately, almost 13,000 soldiers died while imprisoned here. This was mostly due to overcrowding, lack of food, and inadequate shelter. The only way a soldier had a roof over his head was if he were in one of the hospitals or built his own shelter from materials he gathered from the property. Some of the more common shelters were called shebangs. These were tents made from clothing or any other scrap of material they found. The shebangs were useful in keeping the sweltering sun shaded a bit. If you look up on the hill, some shebangs have been reconstructed."

Ellie rooted through her purse for a notepad and paper. "Since we're here, I might as well write up an article for the school paper. Kill two birds with one stone kinda thing."

"Let me call your attention to the deadline," the ranger continued, pointing to a white post about ten feet from where the outer walls would have been. "Any prisoner who crossed the fence line would get shot. Some prisoners even crossed the line intentionally, just to be killed and put out of their misery - hence the name deadline. "

Liam's chest tightened. He struggled to breathe, his vision blurred. It was easy to imagine poor, starving men, half out of their minds with hunger and heat, running over the wooden barricades trying to get shot and hopefully killed, ending their suffering. He could almost feel the desperation closing in like the soldiers must have felt. Liam thought he was going to be sick.

Oh, please, not in front of Ellie. He didn't want to imagine the look on her face if he puked on her tennis shoes. It might even make her drop her piece of gum.

The ranger kept talking. "Stockade Branch is the creek which cuts the prisoner yard in half. This was the main source of water and the only water they had to wash in, as well as drink. Before long, with all of these men using it, the water became fouled and contaminated. Needless to say, this water was the downfall of many imprisoned Union soldiers."

Liam's head was starting to spin. His vision was closing as if he were in a tunnel. The ranger sounded far away.

"Are you okay?"

He looked over towards Ellie and was mildly surprised to see concern on her angelic face.

"No, I don't think I am. I need to go sit down or something. I feel sick."

"I don't doubt it," Ellie said. "With all of the pain and suffering this place has seen, it's filled with such negative energy. I feel it too. It's hard to breathe." She looked at him with a touch of concern in her big, blue eyes, nibbling on her bottom lip while she thought.

Again, Liam looked at Ellie with surprise. Beautiful and smart.

"Rest on the bench over in the shade. If you think you'll be okay, I'm going to catch up with the tour for a few more minutes to get a little more information for the article," she said, tapping her notepad with her pen and blowing a bubble.

Liam nodded. He wanted to clear his head, welcoming a few moments by himself just in case he was going to throw up.

"I'll be back."

Before Liam could answer, Ellie turned and hurried over to the group. He wasn't sure what he had expected by taking a trip to the prison camp, but getting sick while spending the day with a gorgeous girl wasn't it. He was surprised how this place made him feel. It was almost as if he was channeling their spirits and could feel their desperation. What an awful place to live, and an even worse place to take your final breath.

He rested his forearms on his thighs and stared at the ground between his sneakers. He didn't realize Ellie had come back until she thumped down on the bench beside him, startling him.

"Wow. What a horrible place," she said.

"That's what I was just thinking."

"Let's get out of here, and go back to the information center. Maybe they've found something on your mystery soldier."

"Great idea," Liam stood up, more than ready to head back to the information center and away from the desperation of the field.

*****

Back in the cooler, air-conditioned museum, Liam's head cleared and he swallowed the bile back down into his stomach. Each minute back inside he felt much more like himself, and less like an imprisoned Yankee soldier.

"Oh, you're back already. You guys were fast," the ranger said. "I haven't been able to find much, but at least I found him."

She handed Liam a sheet of paper.

"His full name was Nathaniel Greenly. He was from New York and fought with the 7th Artillery, Company M. He was brought here in January of 1865 and the records indicate he escaped in April."

"He escaped? How in the world did anyone escape?"

"There were a little more than 300 soldiers who made their escape from Andersonville. He could have been on a work release program and ran from there or tunneled out under the trees. I couldn't find how he escaped, just that he had. Sorry I don't have anything else for you.

There are some other databases you can check online that may have more information. I wrote down the websites for you. I hope this information helps."

"Thanks," Liam said. "You found out a lot more than I would have."

"I've had much more experience than you, too," the ranger laughed. "Good luck on your project." Another family walked into the museum, she turned to welcome them with a smile.

*****

"Now what do we do?" Liam asked. He and Ellie stopped for a late lunch at a small BBQ place on their way back home. "I mean, where do we go from here?" He stuffed a French fry in his mouth.

Ellie looked at her watch, finishing off her sandwich with a last dainty bite. "Since you don't have Internet, maybe we can make it back to the library before it closes. Hopefully we can find something on one of those websites the ranger gave you."

"What I don't get," Liam said, eating his last fry, "is what happened between the time he escaped from Andersonville in April until the middle of June, when the Whitney's were murdered. Even walking the entire way, it wouldn't have taken six weeks to walk from the prison to Mathisville, would it?"

"There could be a string of unsolved murders all over the area or maybe he didn't have anything to do with the murders. Where did you say you got his name again?"

Thinking fast and not wanting to admit he'd been talking to a ghost, Liam answered, "From Sarah Whitney's diary."

"You found her diary? Where?" Ellie leaned forward on her arms, excited by this new information.

Liam couldn't stop himself from digging an even deeper hole. "I was snooping around in the attic one day and found it in a corner. It was behind some old trunks."

"Awesome. This is way better than extra credit. I'd love to look at it sometime, if it's okay. It'd be so cool to get a view inside the mind of a teenage girl from a hundred and fifty years ago. I'm sure we're not that different. And maybe I'll find some clue you overlooked."

"Sure," Liam said, swallowing hard, wondering how he was going to be able to produce an imaginary diary from Sarah.

Chapter 13

Liam waited to hear from Sarah. He had information, sort of, and he couldn't wait to tell her. After almost a week passed since their last contact, Liam had an idea on how to contact her. Since she wasn't coming to see him in his room, which coincidentally was her old room, she had told him during one of their evening chats, maybe he should try to contact her in her other favorite spot - the sun porch.

As usual, the door was open when it was supposed to be closed against the starless, fall night. Thunder rumbled in the distance, making Liam cringe. He tiptoed in the room and closed the door behind him as quietly as he could so he wouldn't wake his parents. The scent of honeysuckle filled his nostrils. His head swam from the heavy smell.

"Sarah?"

Light giggling filled the room, surrounding Liam with the sound.

"Sarah, I've been waiting for you. I found some information on Mr. Greenly."

"You have? What did you find out?"

"Wait a minute. Before I tell you, how much time do you spend in here?"

"The sun porch?"

"Yes, the sun porch."

"I'm in here most days. It was one of the few places I was happy. Before the war, my mother, sisters, and I would spend our days here. After the war started, we still came out here, but, later, after our chores were done. We would talk, and laugh while we listened to Mother's new music box. I loved to run my hands over the smooth, warm wood. I always dreamed of the day when I would entertain suitors in this cheerful room."

"Is that why the door is always open? Because of you?"

"Yes. It seems one of the best ways of getting your mother's attention, without frightening her."

"My mom? Why do you want my mom's attention?"

"Your mother seems so kind, she reminds me of my own dear mother. She even keeps her music box in the same place Mother kept hers. Oh, how I miss her." Sarah began weeping.

Liam never knew what to do when girls cried, especially a girl who had been dead almost a hundred and fifty years before he was born. He shifted his weight from one foot to another, thinking of a way to make her stop. Changing the subject always seemed to work on his mom.

"What's up with the flowers? I keep smelling them in here but I've never seen them."

"They are wild azaleas, Mother's favorite. She always kept clippings in this room from the first bloom in March until the last one in May. I find the scent comforting."

"So does my mom. The one thing that freaks her out though is when you play the music box."

"I'm sorry. I don't mean to frighten anyone. It helps me remember Mother. It even plays the *Reynardine* the same as Mother's. It was her favorite song."

"But can you not play it when my mom's around though? Hey! That reminds me, when we first moved in I heard someone running up and down the stairs every morning. Was it you?"

"Yes, I was trapped, reliving the day of my death each day, over and over."

"Why did it stop?"

"I'm not sure. The cycle has been broken before, usually as soon as someone realizes I'm here and talks to me, but it begins again as soon as the family leaves. I'm unsure of the rules governing spirits, but I think I have to reenact my last day until I have the attention of someone who lives here. At least that has been the pattern so far. Thank you for acknowledging me. The day of my family's death is not one I care to re-live."

"I can understand that."

"You had said you found out information about Mr. Greenly," Sarah reminded him.

"Oh, right. I almost forgot," Liam admitted. "Give me a minute to think about it again. Oh, yeah. He was pretty young for the war; about 19 years old at the time he escaped from Andersonville, in April, 1865."

"He was imprisoned at Camp Sumter? Are you implying that Mr. Greenly was a...Yankee?"

There was something odd about the tone of her voice. Liam couldn't figure it out. Was she glad Nat Greenly escaped from a horrible war camp or was she upset that her family had taken in a Yankee soldier? Her mood swings wore him out. He never knew which way the conversation was going.

Then he remembered that while the Civil War had been over for more than one hundred and fifty years, the war had just been over for a few weeks when Sarah died. It was still a fresh wound.

"Um, yeah I guess if Mr. Greenly was imprisoned in Andersonville, I mean Camp Sumter, he would be a Yankee."

The lights flickered. Liam started talking fast to distract Sarah from making a scene.

"After he escaped, he disappeared for awhile. The next mention I could find of his name was January 1866, when he married his long time girlfriend, Emma Longstreet. But nine months is a long time. He could have done almost anything during his journey back to New York."

"How can we find out what happened to him during that time? How do we know if he killed my family?"

"I'm working on it," Liam answered. "Oh, you don't by any chance have an old diary, do you?"

"Why?" Sarah sounded suspicious, something dark crept into her voice.

"It's complicated. A girl from school is helping me dig up information on Nat. She asked me where I got his name. I couldn't exactly tell her I've been talking with you; she'd think I was crazy. So I lied. I told her I read it in your diary, which I found in the attic. Now she wants to read it to make sure I haven't missed any clues, and to see how your life compares with hers."

The energy in the room became charged with electricity. Liam shivered from the drastic change.

"As a matter of fact, I do have a diary, but it contains my innermost precious thoughts. I can't just allow anyone to read it."

"I get you want to keep your thoughts secret. But I don't know what to do now. I've lied and been caught. I'm sorta in a tight spot right now too."

"Yes, you are. I fail to see how you becoming a liar is my problem."

This was harder than Liam thought it would be. "Please. Ellie is smart. She might be able to find something leading to the murderer."

"I'm growing weary of this conversation."

The room started warming up again. Liam knew he had one more chance to change her mind. "What if it contains a clue to your family's murders? Can you risk another century of not knowing who did it?"

The temperature in the room returned to normal. Sarah was gone.

Chapter 14

Nat hid behind a tree waiting at the entrance to the tunnel after the sun had dipped below the horizon. With him were the four other men who had spent many sweltering hours hiding from the prison guards and digging with anything they could find: forks and spoons until they broke into too many pieces to use, or canteens after cracks formed and could no longer hold water. Always digging ever closer to freedom, away from this small patch of hell on earth.

None of the men had tried to escape yet. The best they could figure, they would come out well past the stockade and based on the wet earth they dug through, close to a hopefully clean water source, one that would quench their unending thirst and hide their scent from the dogs they knew would be put on their trail.

The men drew straws to see who would brave the tunnel and escape first. Once the first man was successfully through, the other four would quickly follow. If any of the *other prisoners attempted an escape after them, good luck and Godspeed to them.*

Nat drew the longest straw; he would be the first one to drink in the sweet taste of freedom outside of Camp Sumter. As soon as he ducked into the earth tunnel, he heard the cries of crows when they landed on the tree next to the tunnel. He willed them to be quiet; the crows could alert the Rebels to the escape and get the men killed. Nat continued deeper into the earthen tunnel, hoping it would not become his grave. The deeper he crawled, the louder the crows seemed to his ears, as if their cries were amplified to alert the Southern guards.

He broke through the final layer of dirt, making it rain down on him and inhaled the sweet smell of freedom. Free of the hated prison at last! He squeezed through the tight exit, cupped his hands to his lips and cried the call of the Chuck Wills Widow, a bird call he and his Northern brothers had perfected over the last few weeks – alerting his brothers at arms of his successful escape.

No return call met his ears, only the mocking caw of the crows, still creating enough racket to alert the guards. Nat heard muffled yelling; he could hear men shouting, but couldn't decipher the words. In case the tunnel was compromised by the Rebs, he called the lone Chuck Wills

Widow cry again, crossed the gurgling creek and blended in with the dark trees.

The shouting was interrupted by four gunshots: BAM! Obadiah. BAM! Abraham. BAM! Zachary. BAM! Andrew. Four shots – four murders.

Barking dogs coming down the tunnel brought Nat out of his thoughts; he had to run before the dogs reached him. Fighting his way through the blackberry patches and horse nettle, Nat ran hot and bleeding to exhaustion. Knowing he couldn't run any farther, he looked for the largest tree he could climb, pulled himself up, and settled down for a few hours to rest.

Oh, how he despised those murderous crows – they cost the lives of four good, honest men.

After a few hours rest, Nat snuck back out through the night, staying in the darkest shadows, like a panther. He was exhausted, but his hatred of the South and all things southern kept him moving long after his body screamed for rest. He had to get out of this godforsaken place and get back up north. Back to his home and his dear family. Most importantly, back to his beloved Emma.

Even at night this miserable place was hot and sticky. It was so warm and moist in this wretched swamp at times he found it difficult to even take a breath. The ever-present bugs swarmed around his ears, buzzing incessantly. It didn't help to swat at them, he couldn't see them in the darkness anyway. He used what strength he had to hit at the bugs actually biting him. He coughed as one flew into his mouth.

He kept trudging through the soggy Georgia swamp, cursing under his breath the entire time. Why in the world did he fight to keep this repulsive state, or the South for that matter, part of his beloved union? The two parts of the country were worlds apart; they should have kept it that way.

Fighting through the bugs, Nat found himself remembering his time at Camp Sumter. He snorted at the name - 'camp' indeed! Thousands of men confined to so few acres. The stench was suffocating. They were forced to use the same water to drink from which they used to bathe. It's little wonder disease ran through it. Most of the soldiers he served with had either died or turned into walking skeletons covered with filth and vermin. He was one of the few men left from his regiment. Those who managed to survive the disease and the weather still had to contend with the Rebel soldiers. These soldiers acted as their prison wardens, and were supposed to create law and order. The captured Union soldiers were supposed to *receive the same ration of food Rebels received. Hah! The Union troops were lucky if they got fed half-rations, every other day.*

Nat managed to survive both disease and starvation, so he was not about to let himself drop off in some swamp in the middle of nowhere. He was determined to make it back to his home state of New York.

Hatred and bitterness spread though him like the diseases he thought he avoided in the prison. It welled up like bile and left a bitter taste in his mouth. Thinking about the past distracted him from the farmhouse until he almost walked into it. He stopped himself just in time to see the outline of the large house, a darker shadow in the almost moonless night.

Nat backed away from the house, quickly, quietly, before he woke any people inside, or worse, any dogs outside. He snuck back into the woods deciding to wait until morning, when the household woke up and he could get his bearings. At the very least, this family, this Southern family, owed him a meal and a horse if they had one, for what he endured at their Southern prison camp.

Nat felt his hatred growing for everything in the south, man and beast alike.

Chapter 15

Liam found Sarah's small, leather bound diary on his bed. Smiling that he could persuade a ghost to help him, Liam picked up the book and sat on the bed. Since it was Friday night, he figured he had the entire night to stay up and read the diary and would be able to sleep in the next day.

Liam cracked open the diary, feeling the old, hard leather dig into his fingers. He squinted, focusing his eyes. It was hard to decipher Sarah's sketchy, scrawling writing. Even worse, she wrote small and had written on both the front and back of each sheet of paper, so the ink had bled through, making it even more difficult to read. He flipped back to the first page and dropped into Sarah's life.

December 31ˢᵗ – The end of eighteen sixty-four is passing. Die old year, and bring in the peace and joy of a new year. I shall not mourn your passing. You have taken both my dear Father and Brother while leaving the hateful Mr. Whitney in their stead. Oh, dawning New Year, please bring an end to the burden of this war and the hope of new, peaceful days.

January 8th – I overheard Mr. Whitney telling Mother to send me away to the Alabama Insane Hospital to heal my mind. My heart nearly stopped. In this matter Mother does not agree with him. She informs him that I suffer from Melancholy since Father and Brother died. Melancholy and nothing more. Oh, how I do despise that man.

Liam got up to get a pen and paper from his backpack. He would have to Google the word "melancholy" next time he was at the library. He had no idea what it meant, but she definitely sounded depressed to him.

Setting down his notes, he picked up Sarah's diary again.

January 23d – Today we had a party to celebrate the twins' birthday. During this joyous event, Mr. Whitney offered to complete our chores so we could finish the party preparations. An act which caused so much shock I wondered if I had already passed through this earthly life and had entered Heaven's Gates themselves! At the celebration, I sang while Elizabeth accompanied me on the piano and then laughed while I took turns whirling Mary and Louise while they giggled as carefree and happy as they have been in the past year.

February 4ᵗʰ — It's been two years since dear Father's been gone. So much tragedy has happened since that fateful day. Could I have saved him if I had gotten to him quicker? Would that dreadful machine not have trapped his leg if I hadn't called his name? I am tormented daily by the unanswered questions. Oh, what I wouldn't do to bring Father back and send away the dreadful Mr. Whitney. I miss you, Father — please come back.

Liam closed his eyes. Not only did Sarah watch her father die, but she felt she caused his death by calling his name. No wonder she's depressed and has such massive mood swings. He'd probably be a bit crazy himself if it happened to his dad. Poor Sarah.

February 19th – Elizabeth received shocking news today. Her beau, Mr. Jennings was murdered by the Federals during the Battle of Hatcher's Run in Virginia. Mother and I tried to comfort her, but it did little good. Part of her died today as well I fear. I took to the field today to do chores in her stead, so she was able to stay in our room and mourn her lost life with her betrothed. When I went up to fetch her for supper, she had the contents of her wedding hope chest thrown all about the room and was sleeping. I gathered up the linens, smoothed them back out and tenderly placed them back into her trunk. Perhaps in time she will find another to win her heart.

March 8th – I lost time again today. This time Elizabeth found me in the barn, raving mad. She cleaned me up as best she could and tucked me into our bed. When I awoke I knew nothing of the day past breakfast. Why do I not remember what I do? I feel as if there is a demon trapped inside my body, screaming. I need to get it out!

Liam grabbed his paper and made a note to research "losing time". Did it mean she blacked out or just lost track of time?

March 25th – Oh, happy day! I awoke this morning to the sounds of the animals welcoming a new litter of pups into the world! They are the smallest balls of fur I have ever seen. Louise and Mary squealed with delight, holding the pups. Mr. Whitney threatened to drown them all, saying we didn't have enough food to support the family and wouldn't have any to spare for the pups. What an evil man. I will hide them when darkness falls tonight, some place where he will never find them.

April 3d – Mother heard today that the famous phrenologist, Mr. Nelson Sizer will be passing through in a few days. He will meet with interested persons at the town hall in the afternoon, explaining the science behind reading a person's skull to give treatment for mental disorders. After his presentation, Mother will see if he will come to Whitehurst to read my skull to help with my Melancholy and Fits of Rage.

Liam added the word "phrenologist" on his notes. Another word to Google at the library.

April 14ᵗʰ – I had a session with Mr. Sizer, the phrenologist. Mr. Whitney said it was pure bunk and not science so he refused to be in the house. I wonder if Mr. Sizer can move in with us and keep Mr. Whitney away! During the examination, Mr. Sizer measured my head from the forehead to the back of my skull, and then from one ear to the other. He hummed during the entire examination. After measuring my skull he pressed his hands upon the protuberances with a gentle touch and called them by names that meant not a thing to me. He felt my pulse, looked closely at my complexion, and then retired to make his calculations in order to reveal my destiny.

According to Mr. Sizer, I am sensitive, and extremely susceptible to mental and social influences. I have a high degree of nervous activity and will quickly translate my thoughts into actions. I am forcible and determined, also intensely critical; make fine distinctions, keen in my penetrations. I am to have all the sleep I can get, and kept away from excitement. Finally, I will desire to argue the point, and exhibit temper, willfulness, and sarcasm. When this occurs I must be treated in a gentle, considerate manner, and everyone should appeal to my intelligence, pride, and affection, then I should be easily managed. Ha!

Liam tapped his pen against his paper. It sounded as if the phrenologist got Sarah's personality perfectly. Maybe there was hope that if he found out who killed her family, and it turned out not to be Sarah, she would be easily managed. He could hope!

May 6th – It has been one year since I lost my dear brother. Oh, how he is missed. Not a day has passed when I haven't witnessed Mother crying. With Elizabeth mourning her own lost soldier, there has not been much joy at Whitehurst. The twins and I take to the woods whenever we can to escape the unease and sadness surrounding us. It is becoming more and more difficult to get away from Mr. Whitney's watchful eyes.

May 14th – We had a soldier stop through today, Mr. Greenly.

Liam sat up straighter. This is what he was looking for: Nat Greenly.

He was young, about the same age as Brother. Elizabeth seems quite taken with him. It was a sight to see her trying to gain another man's favor. Ever since she lost her own beau, she has been gloomy and cheerless. I was beginning to wonder if another man would ever catch her eye the way Robert had. Based on her actions today, I believe her mourning period has come to an end! The insufferable Mr. Whitney was telling

Mother how difficult it was to feed another mouth – and a half starved man at that. Mother told him to think of her Johnny and they would want some kind family to take in their boy. There was nothing else Mr. Whitney could say.

May 20th – Elizabeth has still been making eyes at her Mr. Greenly but he is not returning her affections. He has been working hard with Mr. Whitney, but is all thumbs. Everything he touches falls apart. Mr. Whitney said we can't expect too much from him being city raised.

Mr. Greenly sure got angry at Elizabeth today. While working in the fields, Elizabeth was out there trying to get his attention. I could not make out the words he said to her since her crying rendered her speech incoherent, but they must not have been kindly. When Elizabeth came back to the house after delivering drinks to both Mr. Greenly and Mr. Whitney, she was in tears. Sometimes Elizabeth tries too hard to make friends and winds up making enemies instead. She's easiest to befriend others when she's behaving as herself. I shall have to ask her about the incident again once she is calm.

May 23d – That snake, Nat Greenly, stole out last night. With him he took Mother's new music box and one of Father's horses. That scoundrel. Even poor, love-struck Elizabeth can't defend him now.

June 8th – The sheriff still has not found Father's horse or Mother's new music box. By now I'm sure thieving Nat Greenly is long gone and our family will never see our possessions again. Only the twins seem untouched by him and his sudden departure.

And then the diary ended. One day before Sarah lost her family, and two days before she lost her own life.

Liam rubbed his dry, tired eyes. He wished he hadn't opened up the diary. It made her life even more real to him. It was one thing to try to solve a mystery for a ghost; it was another to read about her real life, in her own spidery handwriting.

He didn't see any other clues in the diary about the murder and he wasn't about to re-read it. It was too depressing. Maybe Ellie would be able to find something he missed.

Chapter 16

A couple of hours sleeping on the hot swampy ground did little to improve Nat's mood. By the time the sun had risen, so had the family who lived there.

Nat watched as an older woman walked out to the barn all alone. Thinking even if he wasn't welcome, he could fight the woman and win. He was struck with inspiration; he would play his situation off as a Southern soldier making his way back home. With a plan, Nat left his hiding place, and walked toward the first person he had seen in days.

"Hello, ma'am," Nat called out, swallowing the hatred rising in his throat. He waved, trying to appear friendly and unthreatening. "Might you have a meal in exchange for work for a poor, hungry traveler on his way back home from the war?"

"Of course, of course," the woman said, "we welcome all travelers, especially for the Southern boys fighting the good fight. My name is Molly Whitney, and my family

would be delighted to be of service. We don't have a lot of food, as the war has left us poor as well, but you are welcome to what we have. Wash up, while I let my family know you're here."

Molly turned and walked back to the house, alerting her family there was another hungry mouth to feed.

"Benjamin, we have a half starved Rebel heading home outside."

"What are you thinking? Inviting a starving soldier to stay? We have enough food for ourselves, none for yet another starving mouth."

"We're going to be fine. This young man fought for the Southern Cause and is now just trying to get back home. What if this was my boy? We need to help him. We would expect nothing less of other families if we were fortunate enough for Johnny to have been able to come back home to us." Molly sat down and started weeping.

"Blasted war. Bring him in. We will share with him what we have. You're right; we would have expected Johnny to be helped along his way home too, if the war hadn't taken him first."

Molly got to her feet and uncovered the biscuit remnants from breakfast.

When Nat walked into the kitchen, Molly was taken aback, yet again. He was so young, barely a man, to have seen the horrors of war. She was speechless while she served up the last of the eggs and cold buttered biscuits.

Nat felt his skin crawl. While he was washing up, Benjamin Whitney brought him out a change of clothes. His own were torn, tattered, and crawling with bugs that bit him every chance they got. According to Whitney, the clothes belonged to Molly's son, a Rebel soldier who was killed at the Battle of Wilderness. Another dead Rebel – good riddance. So now, here he was sitting in the kitchen of his enemies, wearing their son's clothes. He knew the game he had to play.

"I hope you don't mind, ma'am," he said to Molly. "Your husband gave me your son's clothes. Mine weren't fit to wear anymore."

"I don't mind one bit," Molly replied, choking back tears. "I'm pleased to see the clothes fit you so well. You look to be the same size as my Johnny."

Nat shuddered, but kept the sweet smile plastered to his face. "I'm sorry to hear of your loss." The words were bitter in his mouth.

Chapter 17

Ellie's curly hair bounced as she jumped up and down with excitement Monday at school when Liam handed her the diary during lunch.

On Tuesday, though, Ellie came into the cafeteria without her usual bubble blowing. Her head was down and her perky personality was much more subdued. She had been up all night and hadn't found any other names mentioned in the diary either. She was sad and exhausted. Getting to know Sarah's thoughts and dreams affected Ellie even more than Liam.

"It's so hard to believe someone so vibrant, so full of life, could lose both her family and her own life, all within twelve hours. I grew up hearing about the Whitney murders, and never put a whole lot of thought into them. Since I've read Sarah's diary, I know her mother was deeply distraught over losing her only son, her sister Elizabeth wanted desperately to get married and start her own family, the twins were too young to understand the reasons of the war, but had to live through the desperation and poverty it caused."

Liam thought reading the diary had even affected the way Ellie talked. Who said "deeply distraught" these days?

"And then there was Sarah, documenting the entire thing with some sort of mental trauma, probably from her father dying. The entire time, writing what she saw and felt."

Ellie started pacing around the end of the table. She had picked up a passion Liam had never heard from her before as she continued her speech.

"I know there has always been speculation on whether or not she actually killed her family, based on the violence and force of the blows. Now, after reading her diary, I know for a fact she didn't do it. She didn't have any reason to kill her family. Every teenage girl has something nasty to say about their parents, or hates her siblings for one reason or another. Sarah didn't. Where else to vent those negative and nasty feelings but in a diary? And she didn't. She had nothing but positive, loving things to say about her family. Well, with the exception of her stepfather, but he seemed like a nasty man anyway. But there's no way she did it. She's innocent."

Liam didn't know what to say. He agreed with Ellie. He didn't believe Sarah, even with her mental imbalances, killed her family. The question was, who did?

"Alright," Liam said. "I feel the same way. But how in the world do you find a murderer who committed a crime over one hundred and fifty years ago? I'm sure there wasn't any kind of forensic evidence or police investigation. They found the bodies, Sarah ran, and was killed before they could get any answers. Not to mention, I get the feeling after Sarah's dad died, she had a touch of depression or mental illness. Something just doesn't sit right about all of this."

Ellie's shoulders slumped, deflating like one of her chewing gum bubbles. "You're right. There's no other information about the murders. The only lead is Nat Greenly, but we even hit a dead end with him. No pun intended."

"I know," Liam said, smiling weakly as he remembered his own mistake talking to Sarah. Do you know of any other websites we could check, beside the ones the park ranger gave us?"

"No. But I'll ask my mom today. Why don't you come home with me after school, since I have Internet, and we'll check all our resources again? We can put everything

together and take another look. If we still don't know what
to do, we'll ask Mr. Langford for advice."

Chapter 18

Nat managed to take advantage of the Whitney's hospitality and grieving hearts for a few days. Any opportunity he had to create mayhem, he did; all the while pretending to be an innocent city boy and just plain clumsy. During his short stay he managed to break the plow, take down a portion of the fence, let the livestock loose, and burn a portion of the cotton still in the field.

The Whitneys seemed to overlook the mishaps; since he was a displaced city boy, but Nat knew soon the family would figure out he was doing all of the damage on purpose. Trying to find the most convenient way to leave as well as cause the most damage when he left kept him staying on with the Whitneys long after he should have left, until he had a simple conversation with the eldest daughter, Elizabeth.

He could tell she had her eye on him, and while it repulsed him a southern girl would even consider herself as the same quality of girl as his dear Emma, it had been *awhile since he had the attention of any girl. One day while he and Mr. Whitney were trying to salvage what cotton was left after Nat's latest sabotage, Elizabeth came out with the men's noon meal. Before she had the food out of the basket, the sky darkened, full of crows, all cawing together.*

"That's a bad omen," Nat said.

"What is?" Elizabeth asked, looking at him with hopeful eyes.

"The flock of crows. They announce death."

"Crows don't fly in flocks," Elizabeth said. "Everyone knows a group of crows are called a murder."

Nat felt his blood start to boil and bile rise in his throat. How dare she correct him? Murder of crows, indeed! Who did she think she was? She was an uneducated, backwoods, uppity Rebel supporter. Who was she to tell him what a flock of crows are called? He was educated in one of the finest schools in New York, while she had most likely never seen the inside of a schoolhouse.

Nat snatched the food from Elizabeth's hand, and stormed deep into the scorched field. That night, he woke from his sleeping pallet in the barn, uncovered the mahogany music box he had stolen from the house earlier as a present for his beloved Emma, took one of the Whitney's horses, and vanished.

Chapter 19

After school, Liam was surprised to find he wasn't too uncomfortable in Ellie's ultra-feminine bedroom. There was pink and lace everywhere. Even the laptop they were using to research Nat Greenly was a shade of pink. Liam had never been in such a girly place in his life, but with Ellie sitting next to him, it wasn't too bad. He could be anywhere in the world, and as long as Ellie was beside him, it was a good place to be.

"Okay," Ellie swung around in her pink swivel chair. Chewing her gum, she turned to face Liam, her pink laptop on her knees. "About all we know is on June 3rd, Nat Greenly came through, stayed a few days, wreaked havoc on the farm, had words with Elizabeth and left in the middle of the night with Mrs. Whitney's music box and Mr. Whitney's horse. Now, from what little I know about hearing my dad talk about the law, I think all of this evidence makes Nat Greenly the number one suspect. Even if it is all circumstantial."

"Ellie! Liam! The pizza's here," Ellie's mom yelled from the kitchen. "You'd better come eat while it's hot."

Walking to get their dinner, Liam asked, "But what happened to Nat Greenly between May when he escaped from Andersonville, and January when he married his long time girlfriend in New York?" Liam asked.

"That's the million dollar question," Ellie said. Balancing her slices of pepperoni pizza and Coke in one hand, she grabbed a couple of paper towels for them to share. "There are a couple of websites my mom told me about today. Let's take this back to my room and see what we can find out."

After searching for hours, they still turned up nothing new. Nat Greenly seemed to drop off the face of the earth for eight months: not a single sign of him in cyberspace anywhere.

Chapter 20

A few days after leaving the Whitney plantation, Nat's hatred had poisoned his entire soul. He kept thinking back to Elizabeth's comment and the way she mocked him. Murder of crows. His fallen brothers at Camp Sumter, their escape aborted due to crows. His blood began to boil again. The insects stopped buzzing around him and started whispering, "murder, murder, murder," while the toads croaked, "kill, kill, kill."

It didn't help his state of mind that he was still wearing John Whitney's clothes. The dirty Rebel. How many innocent people, how many Union soldiers had he killed before his own life was lost in battle? Nat couldn't bear to think about it any longer. His thoughts were tormenting him and driving him insane. He knew what he needed to do to quiet his mind – an eye for an eye. He'd make sure the Rebel family would pay for the sins their son had committed, as well as their daughter for making a fool of him.

He turned his horse around and headed back south. A few days later he saw the outline of the Whitney house as the sun was setting. He snuck back into the barn to get a few hours of rest before seeking revenge for all his fallen friends.

Shortly after the moon had risen, Nat stood up, stretched, and searched for a weapon. He found an axe, resting against the side of the barn. He picked it up, testing its weight, and decided it would do the job.

He walked confidently to the front door. He knew the dogs wouldn't bark at him – they knew him and his scent. He grinned in the dark. The family wouldn't know what hit them.

Chapter 21

"Oh, wow. It's after ten," Liam said, stretching his arms over his head and yawning. "Time flies when you're researching dead people. I need to be getting home." He grabbed up their dirty paper plates and headed for her bedroom door.

"You're right, it really is late." Ellie yawned, looking at her watch. "I'll take those," she motioned towards the plates, "and walk you out."

Liam pedaled home as fast as he could, zooming down the dark, deserted streets. He flew into his driveway at 10:18. Liam's heart sank when he saw a police car.

Fearing his worst nightmares were coming true in the haunted house, Liam rode his bike up to the front steps. He took the porch steps two at a time. His heart pounded against his chest as he threw open the screen door, panicked something horribly wrong had happened to his parents.

"Oh, Liam," his mom exclaimed, as she jumped up off the couch and grabbed him into a suffocating hug. "Where have you been?"

"I've been over at Ellie's house, researching our project," he said. "Why are the cops here?"

"For you, son." Liam had never seen his dad without a smile, but he didn't have one now. Dad readjusted his glasses. "When you didn't get off the bus, we called the library. You weren't there. We called the school. You weren't there. When you didn't come home for dinner, we started getting worried. When it got dark, we called the police. Do you know what time it is?" His dad's voice had been getting louder as he talked. The last question was almost a shout.

"I do now," Liam looked at his feet. "I just realized it was after ten and got here as quickly as I could."

"You couldn't pick up a phone and call us?" his dad bellowed, nervously adjusting his glasses again.

Liam's public embarrassment was interrupted by the police officer. "Since you're home, safe and sound now, we'll be leaving." They packed up their notes and paperwork, handed Liam's mom back the picture she had given them, and left the house.

"You are in so much trouble, young man. Go to your room. I can't even talk to you right now. Think about what you have done to your mother and me. I'll figure out your punishment later; when I'm not so mad," his dad said, still fussing with his glasses.

Chapter 22

Life was tough for Liam the next few days. At first his parents didn't speak to him, just left him to wonder what his punishment would be.

Then the sentence came down.

He wasn't able to leave the house without his parents, except to go to school, for the next two weeks. One of his parents would even pick him up and drop him off at school; both his bike and skateboard were on lock-down. He also had to do all the chores around the house, including thoroughly cleaning the house from top to bottom. He was miserable, but knew once his parents calmed down he might be able to end his prison term early because of good behavior.

After school one afternoon, he was vacuuming his mom's office when he noticed her filing cabinet drawer was open. He saw his mom's organized files, each person on the family tree had their own folder and tab sticking up for easy access. His eyes landed on the name Emma

Longstreet. The name seemed familiar. Where had he seen it before?

His curiosity got the better of him, so he turned off the vacuum and grabbed the folder, scanning the pages. He saw Emma Longstreet was married to none other than Nathaniel Greenly. A shiver ran down his spine. Liam's knees turned rubbery. He sat on the edge of the desk and read his family tree closer.

Liam was in shock. There it was in black and white. Nathaniel Greenly was his mother's great, great grandfather, which meant Nathaniel Greenly was his great, great, great grandfather.

"Mom," Liam yelled, running down the stairs. "Mom!"

He skidded to a stop at the bottom of the steps, missing running into his mom by inches, as she was carrying laundry upstairs.

"What's this?" He waved the folder in her face.

"I don't know. What is it?" She set the laundry basket on the bottom step and grabbed his hand, stopping the waving papers.

"This is my family tree. Our family tree," she explained. "Why? What's the big deal? I was working on it this morning."

"You know the soldier I'm doing the research on?" Liam asked.

"Oh, yeah. The research that made you forget to call your parents and let us know where you were or that you were still alive. The research that got you grounded until your twenty-first birthday? Yes, I'm familiar with it."

Ignoring Mom's sarcasm, Liam continued. "This name right here," he said, pointing to Nathaniel Greenly's name with such force he almost poked a hole in the paper. "This is the soldier I'm researching."

"Really? Are you sure this is the same guy and not someone with the same name?"

"What are the odds?" Liam asked. "All I know is that he's from New York; which is where you're from, and he married a woman named Emma Longstreet in 1886."

He showed his mom the paper again.

"As weird as all this seems, you might be right. I have more information about him in my office," she said, pushing past Liam, reading the family tree on her way up the stairs.

She rifled through her filing cabinet. "Here it is," she said, pulling out a manila folder and waving it victoriously, "Emma Longstreet - Nathaniel Greenly."

She laid the folder on her desk and opened it. On top of the skinny file was a copy of an old black and white photo of an unhappy looking young man.

"Here he is."

It was strange. Liam was able to put a face with the name that had haunted him for weeks. Not only that, they were related. How in the world would he be able to tell Ellie this weird twist? How would he tell Sarah?

His mom handed him the manila folder. "Are you still sure it's the same guy?"

Liam knew, without a doubt, his ancestor was the mystery man he had been searching for. "Was he a Union soldier in the New York Artillery? Captured during battle and kept as a prisoner of war housed at Camp Sumter?"

Liam and his mom didn't say anything for a few moments. They just stared, unblinking, at one another. His mom broke the silence.

"What are the odds?" she asked, rubbing the goose bumps on her arms.

*****

Liam took the folder to his room in order to investigate the contents and read it in private. Nathaniel Greenly was born in Broome County, New York on April 14, 1846. He joined the New York 7th Artillery, Company M to fight against the Confederacy as soon as they would take him. His military career was short lived. He fought a few battles before he was captured at Cold Harbor, Virginia, and then was confined at Camp Sumter. There was no mention of his escape, just that he married his childhood sweetheart, Emma Longstreet.

After his years as a soldier, Nathaniel worked in the family business, running a dry goods store. He and his wife had eight children, one of which was Martha, Liam's great, great grandmother, the only daughter to be married. Is that who his mother's music box came from? Is it the same old wooden music box that is sitting on the shelf in the sun porch? The one Sarah plays?

Liam turned over the last sheet of paper. That was it. Nothing about what kind of person he was or what he did with his life, aside from working in the family's dry goods store and raising eight children.

Liam was disappointed. There were just facts surrounding the man. As he had so recently found out by knowing Sarah, people from the past are so much more than boring facts and details. They had lives with emotional ups and downs. They were human too.

"Mom?" Liam yelled, as he left his bedroom and headed back towards his mom's office. "Mom!"

"What?" She poked her head out of the doorway. "What are you yelling for? It's just the two of us, and I'm right here."

"Is this all the information you have on him?"

"Everything I have is in the folder I gave you. Why? Didn't you find anything interesting?"

"No. I was hoping for more. Like his hopes and dreams. That kinda thing."

"Sorry, I don't have anything like that. But you know, Grandma might. She's lived in the old farmhouse her entire life. I think it's the same house Nat Greenly built for his family after the war. I'll check with her. If she has anything, maybe she'll let you dig through it when we go visit for Christmas."

"Speaking of Grandma, where did she get her music box?"

"Mine? The one in the sun room?" His mom asked. "I'm not sure which woman in the family originally had it. The song it plays was popular during the Civil War. Let me see the family tree again."

"According to the date, the first woman in the family after the war was Emma Longstreet," his mom said.

"Again, maybe Grandma will have more information. This is getting way too bizarre."

Liam had forgotten they were making the trip to New York for the holidays. Now thinking about being snowed in for days without TV or any friends to talk to didn't sound so bad. The only thing he had to decide was if he should tell Ellie or Sarah that Nat Greenly, the man who possibly murdered the entire Whitney family, was his great, great, great grandfather. Things could be a little awkward if he told them too soon, before he knew for sure.

Chapter 23

Liam's grandma was not like most of his friends' grandparents. Sure, like other grandparents, she was old and had graying hair, but that's where the resemblance ended. Liam liked to think of her as an aging hippie. She loved spending time outside with nature. She believed in bringing nature inside, but not in a dirty, filthy sort of way. She always had whatever flowers and greenery were in season in vases all over the house. Her furniture was made from various pieces of wood and then covered in her hand-made quilts. All of her dishes and anything resembling a bowl were made of clay from a local potter. She grew most of her own vegetables, had a cow and a goat for milk and butter, and chickens for eggs. If she could ever kick her love of bacon and become a vegetarian, she would be totally self-sufficient.

She also lived in the Adirondacks in upstate New York which was so different from anywhere he had ever spent time. The house was perfect - a two story farmhouse with mountains in the backyard and a sparkling clear stream running through the front yard. It had always been a special place, even more so now under a magical blanket of snow. Liam was transported into a true winter wonderland when he visited his grandma in December for Christmas.

Caught up in all the winter delights, Liam put Nat Greenly on the back burner. He was exploring all the activities he could never experience living in Florida: skiing, snow boarding, and his new favorite, snowmobiling. Finding out if he had a murderer in the family could wait a little longer.

Toward the end of his visit, Liam's grandma caught him in the kitchen while he was making himself a snack of leftover Christmas turkey.

"There you are. Your mom said you are working on a project for school."

Liam looked at her like a deer caught in headlights. His eyes were wide and confused. Weeks had gone by since he last thought of school so he had a difficult time processing what his grandma was saying. Then a name clicked in his mind: Nat Greenly.

"Oh, yeah," Liam mumbled, mouth full of turkey sandwich. He finished chewing, swallowing hard, almost choking on the dry mouthful. "This house," he started, "was built by Nat Greenly, wasn't it?"

"It was, even though I've never heard anyone refer to him by anything other than Nathaniel. I swear you kids abbreviate everything nowadays."

Correcting himself, but ignoring his grandma's comment, "Do you know anything about Nathaniel? Do you have any photos? Diaries? Anything?"

"I'll be honest, I'm not sure what all I have on him. I know a couple of things about the man: he built a phenomenal house, which I've been fortunate enough to call home my entire life, had lots of kids, and made some sort of a confession on his deathbed."

"Confession? What did he confess?" Liam was watching his grandma's reaction closely. "What did he do? Cheat on his wife? Steal something? Murder? What was it?"

"It's funny you should mention murder. Nathaniel was a soldier during the Civil War and it seems the war took a toll on him emotionally. Many soldiers did things they wouldn't normally do in non-war situations. Anyway, as the story goes, on his deathbed, he wanted to confess his war crimes to the family priest, but since it was January, they were snowed in. He confessed to the only family member still living at home at that time, his daughter Eleanor. It's my understanding she wrote it all down in order to give it to the priest to save Nathaniel's soul."

"What did he say?" Goose bumps popped up on Liam's arms as a small shiver ran down his spine.

"I don't know. I've never had any desire to read about the horrific things war makes men do, especially my own ancestor. I've been quite content all these years thinking positive things about the man who built this house and the families who have lived here."

"Oh," Liam sighed, disappointed at being so close to finding out the truth.

"But I have everything up in the attic if you'd like to know what tortured Nathaniel's soul into a deathbed confession. Just do me a favor, don't tell me what you find."

"Deal! Can you show me where everything is?"

"Absolutely," Liam's grandma said as she gathered herself up from the bar stool across from him. "Follow me."

Liam followed his grandma up two flights of stairs to the third floor of the house. They stopped outside the small, closed door leading to yet another flight of stairs to the attic.

"Are you sure you want to know?" his grandma asked, holding onto the doorknob. "Once you find out the truth, you can't pretend you don't know anymore."

"I'm ready," he answered, as he ducked under the low doorway, leading the way up the narrow attic steps.

The air was noticeably colder in the attic. Liam attributed the cold temperature more to the snow outside and lack of heating up there than the ghostly experiences he had at home with Sarah.

"In this corner is Nathaniel's trunk." Grandma said, pulling her long wool sweater around her against the cold. "And here is Eleanor's trunk. I have never looked through either one. You are more than welcome to look through both. I'm not sure which one the confession will be in."

Liam grabbed the trunk belonging to Nat Greenly. He tried to pick it up, but the trunk was so heavy; Liam struggled and grunted, but the trunk didn't move. "What do you have in here, a body?"

"It might be easier to slide the trunk towards you," his grandma suggested. "And there's no telling what's in there. Since getting it down out of the attic doesn't appear to be an option, you'll have to look through it up here. Put on a jacket first, though. It's freezing."

"Do you have the keys for the trunks?" Liam asked.

"Seriously? I just told you I've never looked through either of them. What in the world makes you think I'd have the keys?"

"I had to ask."

Liam looked at the old, leather-covered trunks with their dusty, pitted locks and doubted he would be successful at opening them or finding their secrets. How could he get this close and still not know?

"Here, try this," his grandmother handed him a hair pin she had just taken out of her graying hair.

Liam looked over at his grandmother, shock spreading across his face.

"What? There's a reason people try hair pins in movies to open locks. They work."

"And how would you know?"

"I haven't always been a doddering old lady. I've had some excitement in my youth." She smiled. "Scoot over. Let me show you how it's done."

Liam slid over to the side, letting his grandmother tackle the old trunks and their rusty locks. After just a few seconds of watching his grandmother fiddle her hair pin in the lock, twisting it around, he heard a definite *CLICK*.

His grandmother winked. "Let's keep those lock picking skills our little secret, shall we?"

*****

Settled down, with both trunks open in front of him, wearing his winter coat, hat, scarf, and gloves, Liam got to work. He grabbed handfuls of papers out of Nat's trunk first, his hands tingling while he thought of his ancestor touching the same papers. Liam would finally find out, one way or another, if Nat was responsible for murdering the Whitney family.

Liam took a deep breath, hesitating. His grandma was right though, whatever he learned, he wouldn't be able to forget. What should he do? Liam felt as if he were standing at a doorway. Should he open the door and walk through, or turn and walk away, leaving history undisturbed? Liam knew there was only one choice he would be content with. He opened the door to the past and entered.

Liam honestly believed the confession would be right on top. His fingers would magically go right to it, and he would learn Nat's deepest secret. He also thought everything he read would be interesting, even earth-shattering. He was wrong on both counts. After searching for what felt like hours in the freezing cold, but which his watch revealed was only about fifteen minutes, Liam leaned back and closed his eyes, wondering why on earth anyone would want to keep such boring stuff, like daily receipts for the store and the farmhouse.

Realizing the information wouldn't find itself, Liam straightened up and resumed his search with renewed determination, hoping he would find something interesting and wasn't turning into a human popsicle for no reason.

The deeper into the truck Liam dug, the more interesting it became. There were locks of hair from the children, each tied in a different color ribbon. Liam found receipts from when the house was built and marveled over how inexpensive it was to live back then. He found flowers which had been pressed flat, but those disintegrated in his fingers as soon as he tried to pick them up. He discovered romantic notes Emma had written to Nat, embarrassed by the flowery, romantic poetry. Then his fingers scraped the bottom of the trunk. That was it. The trunk was empty. Nothing to show Nat was the monster Liam believed him to be. Maybe Nat didn't commit the crimes after all. Before giving up on the trunk, Liam knocked and thumped on every side, just to be sure nothing had been over looked, hoping there was a false bottom or side concealing the confession. Nothing.

Liam sighed and began to repack the trunk, looking though everything a second time just to make sure. There weren't any earth shattering discoveries the second time though either. Frustrated, Liam turned his attention to Eleanor's trunk.

Instead of spending time reading each and every document, Liam skimmed over the items in the trunk. Nothing in here either. Realizing he needed to slow his search, he read each and every document before he placed it back in Eleanor's trunk. Still nothing. Making sure he investigated every inch of the trunk, he thumped every square inch on the outside of the trunk, but nothing echoed back, nothing hollow. Just as he was getting ready to close the trunk and abandon his search, Liam noticed the fabric on the inside of the lid was peeling up in the corner.

Looking behind him to make sure his grandma wasn't sneaking up on him, ready to chastise him for taking apart the trunk, he peeled back the fabric. When he had peeled back enough material to get a glimpse of the treasure hiding inside he saw a stack of old, yellowing pages tied together with a black ribbon. He pulled the crisp pages free, careful not to destroy them.

The top page, written in hard to read, scrawling handwriting were the words:

Papa's Confession

January 22d 1918

Chapter 24

Liam held off reading the confession until the suspense was ready to kill him. He took them downstairs. He knew whatever those papers revealed, his life would somehow be different, plus grandma had asked him to help cook dinner and he couldn't read the papers in front of her. As he buttered the garlic bread, he thought how he was about to enter the mind of his great, great, great grandfather. He wanted to hold onto this thought of not knowing what happened one hundred and fifty years ago as long as he could.

After he and his family had dinner, and after they had played round after round of his grandma's favorite dice game, Farkel, Liam knew he was ready. His family had gone to bed; he had the entire, deathly quiet house all to himself. He made himself a cup of hot chocolate and went to the living room of the house Nat Greenly himself had built. It didn't seem right, somehow, to read the confession in the harsh lighting of electric lights; so Liam lit some of

161

his grandmother's hand-dipped herbal candles, stoked the fire in the fireplace, turned off the lights, and settled down next to the fire. Turning to the first page, Liam adjusted his eyes to the scrawling writing, and began to read.

I, Eleanor Greenly, am recording the confession of my father, Nathaniel Greenly, on his deathbed, in order to free his tormented soul and allow him to receive the forgiveness of our Lord in order to enter the Kingdom of Heaven. What follows are Father's own words.

I, Nathaniel Greenly, being of sound mind and body, need to confess of a crime I committed while in my youth, during the War of Southern Aggression. My young age is no excuse for the crime I committed, nor is the fact I had just escaped as a captive from a prisoner of war camp and heard the others in my party murdered in cold blood by the rebels. For there are never any excuses for the crime of murder.

I developed a hatred for the southern rebels during the war. I didn't understand their motives and desires as I'm sure they didn't understand mine. The more men I saw die in battle, the more lives wasted because of war, the deeper my hatred became.

When my regiment was captured, we were held as prisoners of war on the smallest wasteland imaginable, our own version of hell on earth: Camp Sumter. Existence there was barely living at all. Union soldiers were still dying all around me, this time from starvation, disease, or the cruel treatment of our rebel captives.

Thankfully I was confined for just a short period of time. I joined forces with four other captives and set forth into digging a tunnel to our escape. As luck would have it, I was the first through the tunnel. The others were captured and based on their intent to escape were all shot on the spot. I alone made it out that night. The caws of the crows murdered my Union brothers.

To escape the dreaded south that wanted me dead, I started my long journey, walking home to New York. Not being as smart as I thought, I became twisted and turned around on more than one occasion. Weeks after leaving Camp Sumter, I was still walking around the swamps of Georgia. As misfortune would have it, I came across the farmhouse of the Whitney family.

Liam's blood turned to ice as he read those words, and the candle light flickered eerily across the page. He looked around the room to make sure he was still alone. When he didn't see or sense anything else, his eyes drifted back to the paper.

They were cordial and generous, giving me food when they themselves didn't have much to eat, most likely due to the fact I had impersonated a lone Rebel soldier trying to return home. They welcomed me to stay as long as I liked, even replacing my tattered rags with clothes from their own son, whom they lost in that dreadful war. In my hatred and bitterness, I didn't realize at the time how kind these people were; All I could see is they were a southern family, and therefore my enemy.

I tried everything I could think of to sabotage the family's farm: I let animals loose, dropped the bucket down the well, and caught their only source of money, their meager cotton crop, on fire.

The eldest daughter, Elizabeth, seemed taken with me and flirted with me every opportunity she had. My heart was already claimed by my dear Emma and while Elizabeth was quite pretty, she was a southern girl.

Liam looked up, staring into the candle flame, unable to understand the passions that ran on both sides of the Civil War. It happened so long ago. But to Nathanial Greenly it was a defining moment in his life, and to Sarah it was still fresh. Liam shifted in the chair to burrow deeper into the cushions before continuing.

One day, I was helping Mr. Whitney work in the field. Elizabeth came down, bringing beverages to cool her father and me in the June heat. Another unfortunate incident happened, I looked up and commented on the flock of crows flying overhead – an ominous sign, thinking back to the flock that alerted the Rebels to our escape and ultimately killed four good men.

When I said something about the flock, Elizabeth giggled, telling me a group of crows was called a murder, not a flock. I'm not sure what made me angrier, a beautiful girl laughing at me, correcting me in a sense, or the fact the crows had found me once more. I'll admit I was quite arrogant in my youth, and rarely felt I was wrong. I didn't like to be laughed at or corrected and over reacted to her flirtatious comment.

In my anger, I stole out in the middle of the night. Before I left, I took Mrs. Whitney's music box as a gift for my beloved Emma, as well as one of Mr. Whitney's horses to ensure quicker flight to the north.

A few days out, still enraged by Elizabeth's flirtatious comment, the word 'murder' kept creeping back into my brain. Like a man caught in the grip of fever, I could think of nothing else. I turned the horse around and headed back to Georgia, and the Whitney's farm.

In the middle of the night I found myself back at the Whitney farmhouse. I spotted an axe, resting by the

Whitney's woodpile, and walked into the farmhouse, knowing it would not be locked.

My own sense of self-preservation must have taken over as I do not recall the gruesome details that followed. I'm not making excuses for my actions, but I am thankful I cannot remember them. I saw enough of the carnage to know I murdered the entire family as they slept in their beds, as I was covered in their life's blood.

Realizing what I had done, I hid the axe in the rafters in the barn, stole another horse, as the one I had originally taken was suffering from exhaustion, and rode away with the devil on my tail. I have not felt more than a single moment's peace since that horrific, fateful night.

I am an old man now, taking my last breaths. I can look back at my life and see what kind of person I was. I am by no means proud of my actions, but rather needed to get them off my chest before my earthly life is finished. While I was never held accountable for my actions by courts here on earth, I know I will be judged by a higher court. May God have mercy on my soul.

Within moments of uttering the last sentence, my father fell into a deep sleep, exhausted. He died in his sleep three hours later, never once waking. May he at last be able to rest in peace.

Liam noticed his hands were shaking, so he rested the old, crisp papers on his lap. He closed his eyes and shook his head. Nat did it after all. The axe, the murder weapon that was never found, might even still be in the barn. Shaking, he brought his cup of hot chocolate to his lips, not noticing it had long since turned cold.

Chapter 25

Liam's head was still spinning when he got back home from his grandma's in New York. What was he going to tell Ellie about his trip? More important, what was he going to tell Sarah? He decided the first thing he wanted to do was grab a flashlight and head out to the old barn to see if he could find the axe. He didn't expect to find it, but he had to look.

Trying to pull open the rotten door was the first sign this wasn't going to be easy. Grunting and straining against the door, Liam felt like an idiot when he looked down and saw no amount of tugging would open the door: the ground had built up over the bottom of the door, it would take a shovel and a couple of hours to be able to go in through the door.

Taking his dad's recommendation to heart to "work smarter, not harder," Liam wandered around the outside of the barn, looking for another entrance. He found a low window with all of the glass knocked out, so there was no risk of slicing himself open as he crawled through.

Sitting on the window ledge, Liam turned on his flashlight to scan the floor below before he jumped down. He saw old, rusted farm tools leaning against the walls, but nothing except tons of dirt on the floor below. He landed harder than he thought he would and his ankles buckled, dropping him to his hands and knees.

Glad no one was around to see that, he stood up, brushing himself off. The impact turned the flashlight off, but after beating it against his hand, it came on; a little dimmer than before. Liam thought back to the confession. Nat said he hid the axe in the barn's rafters.

Liam scanned the ceiling, half expecting to see the axe head sticking out. He didn't. He scanned the barn looking for a ladder or something that might work to get him closer to the ceiling and the rafters. Nailed to the side of the barn was a crude wooden ladder which was probably used years ago to get up to the hay loft when the barn held livestock. Some of the rungs were broken, but Liam didn't think it would slow him down much. He was surprised how sturdy it was. It seemed better built than the new ladder his dad bought last weekend.

Even though the temperatures were cool, Liam was sweating from exertion, pulling himself up the dusty rungs. By the time he reached the floor of the former hay loft, sweat had trickled down his face and arms, leaving trails in the dirt on his skin. His mom would kill him if she saw how dirty he was. No time to worry about it now. It was time to find the murder weapon.

Liam tried to put himself into his ancestor's mind. If he had just murdered an entire family and wanted to hide the weapon, where would he hide it? Figuring getting out quickly was important, the best spot to hide something would be next to the ladder; assuming the ladder was in the same spot all these years.

With at least a place to start looking, Liam hoisted himself up by the rafters near the ladder. It was too dark to see anything. Putting the flashlight handle in his mouth, Liam pulled himself back up, this time his forearms screaming from the exertion they weren't used to. Holding himself up, he moved his head back and forth, scanning the rafters with light.

His arms started shaking and Liam knew he didn't have much longer before he had to let go and drop back down. This might be the last chance he had to look for a while. Scooting his fingers down the beam, he tried to find a different angle to see from. His right pinky touched something cool and hard.

Excited and about to lose his grip, he grabbed for the object with his right hand, letting go of the rafter and falling the couple of feet to the hay loft. With his feet firmly on the ground, Liam opened his fingers. A lone, rusty axe head. The handle had either broken or rotted off years ago and the metal on the axe head was pitted and dull either from years of neglect and rust or hard work and blood. With his limited crime scene knowledge, it was hard to tell. He shuddered thinking he could be touching the blood of victims from a murder over one hundred and fifty years ago.

After looking at it in the dim light of the barn he dropped it to the ground, not wanting to try to hold onto it and climb back down the old ladder. Safely on the ground, Liam grabbed the axe head, wrapped it in the bottom of his shirt, and took off for the house, in desperate need of a shower.

*****

After he got cleaned up and hid the axe under his bed until he could show Ellie, he felt the temperature drop.

Goose bumps appeared all over his arms, and he could see his breath: Sarah.

"Liam, you have returned."

"I have."

Sarah giggled, "I missed you. Where have you been?"

Thinking she meant where he had been for the last two weeks, not that he had just searched the barn for the murder weapon, he went with the easiest answer. "I went to my grandma's for Christmas."

"Oh." Her voice made her sound as if she were pouting. "And here I was all by myself for Christmas. Alone, again."

Good grief. Her moods changed faster than popcorn in a microwave.

Giggling again, "I was hoping you were busy finding out who murdered my family."

Liam chickened out and decided he wasn't ready to tell Sarah yet. "No, sorry. I haven't learned anything new since I left."

He instantly hated himself for lying to her.

"Liam…"

"Yes, Sarah?"

"Why are you lying to me?"

Liam swallowed hard.

"I can always tell when you are lying; you close your eyes."

His skin prickled with sweat. Busted!

Liam sighed, dreading the upcoming conversation. "Okay then, I have some information for you."

"You do?" Hope was evident in Sarah's voice, replacing the tone of moments before, catching Liam off guard again.

He shook his head to clear his thoughts. "I know who killed your family."

"You do," she repeated. "Who was it?"

"Nat Greenly."

"That treacherous snake," she said, with venom in her voice.

The lights flickered. A hot, sick feeling enveloped him. "How did you find out?"

Taking a deep breath, Liam rushed through the explanation. "I found his deathbed confession. He details almost everything in it; your family's kindness, and his hatred of everything southern."

"Why did he do it? Did he say that?"

"Sort of. He blamed the war for changing him, making him despise the south and everything southern; his sworn enemies. It didn't help when your sister Elizabeth laughed at him."

"She did? I don't remember her laughing at him."

"You wrote about it in your diary. Elizabeth brought drinks out to your father and Nathaniel, when they saw a group of crows fly overhead. He said it was a bad omen to see a flock of crows. Your sister corrected him, saying they were called a murder of crows, not a flock."

"Is that what she said to him? Elizabeth never told me the words they exchanged. She ran back to the house, crying, saying he was quite angry with her."

"You're right, he was very angry with her. When she corrected him, something inside him kinda snapped. He left that night. The more he thought about what she said, the angrier he became until he turned around and came back to the house. What's weird is he knew he did it, admitted to it, but doesn't remember a single detail about committing the murders. He regretted the whole thing on his death bed."

"Regrets won't bring my family back, will they?" Her voice was ice.

"You're right, it won't bring them back. But does it matter at all that it tormented him every day of his life?"

"No, it does not. His thoughtless actions have tormented me every day of my death. He lived, my family didn't." Liam could feel a charge in the air, electrifying the room. "Why do you care if he felt remorse, if he was tormented? What does it matter to you?" With each sentence her voice became louder until she was screaming.

Liam took a deep breath. He had to tell her. "Because he's my great, great, great grandfather." The words came rushing out like a flood. He wished he could take them back as soon as they spilled from his mouth.

Everything in the house grew silent. It almost seemed as if the house were holding its breath, too, waiting to see how Sarah would react.

"What?" Her voice was low and quiet. Liam thought it sounded more like a growl than a spoken word.

Liam squinched his eyes closed, he didn't want to say it again.

"What did you say?" she repeated.

It felt as if all the air had been sucked out of the room.

Liam wished he had made something up. Anything would be better than telling a ghost with a loose grip on sanity that he was related to the man who murdered her family. He felt he had no other choice if he was going to be able to breathe again. His voice squeaked as he told her, "He's my great, great, great grandfather."

As soon as the words left Liam's lips, the house exploded. Liam learned it's one thing to upset a girl; it's another to upset a ghost.

Sarah started howling an unearthly wail. It was a cross between hurricane winds ripping though the house, and the screams of a tormented cat, with a touch of a wolf's lonely howl. Every light flickered until the bulbs exploded. Each smoke alarm screamed like it had the first night the family moved in to the house. The doors all slammed shut at once. Liam felt the hairs rise all over his body, from the top of his head, down his neck, to his arms, and down to his toes.

A loud boom shook the floor under his feet. Downstairs, his mother screamed.

Fumbling in the dark, he rushed to open his bedroom door.

"Mom! Dad!" he screamed, running into the hallway. "Where are you?"

"I'm down here," his mom answered. "What's going on? Are you okay?"

"I'm fine. I'm coming downstairs. Where's Dad?"

Liam thought he heard his dad reply, but over the ghostly screaming and wailing, he wasn't sure.

As he ran down the stairs, his foot hit something solid, and in the dark, Liam tripped and tumbled down, rolling all the way to the landing.

Breath knocked out of him, Liam laid flat on his back for a few seconds, the house screaming around him. He moved his hands, they weren't broken. Not wasting any more time, he rolled over to his stomach, pushing himself up, noting his arms weren't damaged either. Wincing when he pushed himself to his feet, his ankle feeling more tender and sprained than broken, he squinted in the darkness, gathering his bearings.

He heard a low moan.

"Dad? Is that you?"

"Uuuggghhh."

Liam scrambled back up the stairs, feeling each step with his fingers before crawling up. He touched something warm and sticky. Snatching his fingers back, he brought them to his nose. The metallic smell of blood.

"Dad?"

"Uuuggghhh," his dad started to move, trying to sit up.

"Don't move. I'm gonna go get Mom."

"Liam," his mother yelled, trying to be heard over the ghostly sounds in the house. "What's going on? I can't see anything. Where are you?"

"Here on the stairs. I tripped over Dad. He's hurt. I think he might be unconscious."

Before Liam could get to his feet, Mom was beside him. She put a hand on Liam's back.

"I'm right here," she said. "Are you alright?"

"I think so. It's Dad I'm worried about."

"We have to get out of this house. I'm not sure what's going on, but we need to leave."

Liam had never heard his mom talk as calmly as she did right now. She was in complete control; a mother taking care of her family.

"Hook your arm under your dad's and I'll get this side. Carefully lift him up. You okay? Do you have his weight? Alright, slowly take a step down the stairs. That's it. Now another."

Painstakingly, Liam and his mom got his dad out of the dark screaming house. When they reached the front door, it wouldn't open. Liam's heart dropped. Was Sarah so angry she wouldn't let them leave? When he tugged forcefully on the door again, it released and swung open.

Liam and his mom half walked, half dragged his dad to the car. Liam opened the back door, and together, they slid his dad onto the back seat.

"We need to get him to the hospital," Mom said.

"I know, his head's bleeding. I touched it. He had already fallen when I tripped over him on the stairs. I didn't see him."

"Well, how could you?" Mom felt under the car seat for the spare key. "All the lights blew out. And that horrible sound...." She found the key and started the car. "What happened?"

"Let's get out of here first, then I'll tell you everything I know. It is one crazy story."

*****

Liam told the short version of the long ghost story on the way to the emergency room. For the first time ever, Mom was speechless. She'd surprised him twice in the last half hour. They rode the last mile to the hospital in silence. Pulling up to the emergency entrance, his mom found her voice.

"What do we do now?"

"Get Dad out of the car."

The next few hours were a whirlwind of activity. Liam's dad was going to be all right. During Sarah's temper tantrum, something hit him in the head, knocking him out. Since he was trying to get downstairs when the lights went out, he fell the first few steps, breaking his arm in the process. Liam's kick didn't break anything else, but left a huge black and purple bruise on his back. Since he had a concussion, the hospital wanted to keep him for twenty-four hours, to make sure there were no complications.

While Liam and his mom waited for his dad to wake up, Liam borrowed his mom's phone, went outside and called Ellie. He was surprised when his call went directly to voicemail. He left a message to let her know he was back from his trip to New York, but was now at the Emergency Room; his dad had an accident but the doctors were expecting him to be all right.

Liam walked back into the waiting room, disappointed he wasn't able to talk to Ellie. Flipping through magazines, Liam was caught off guard when he heard a female voice call his name.

"Liam? Are you in here?"

He cautiously raised his head and looked around. For a split second, he thought Sarah had found him. But he was wrong. The voice was Ellie's!

Liam jumped to his feet, never so happy to see her bouncy blonde curls as he was at that moment. She turned around, chewing on her bottom lip and spotted him in the empty room and rushed over.

"Hey!" Ellie grabbed Liam in a hug. "I tried to call you back, but your phone just rang and rang."

Liam looked at his mom's phone and just as he suspected, no bars in the hospital.

"You sounded upset. I wanted to make sure everything was okay."

Liam cracked a small grin. She had come to see him. And hugged him.

"Anyway, how's your dad? What happened?"

"He bumped his head," Liam said flatly.

Ellie looked into his eyes, searching for more of an explanation. When she didn't see any, she looked at Liam's mom for answers. Ellie's lips were squeezed together, and she'd stopped chewing her gum. Her eyes squinched up, letting him know she didn't believe a word he said.

"Well," his mom started, a pained look on her face.

"Oh, all right," Liam admitted, looking over at his mom, saving her the explanation. "I'll tell you the truth, but you have to promise to stay and listen to the entire story."

Ellie looked confused. "Okay. I promise."

Liam was glad his mom was there to help him tell Ellie the bizarre story. Liam felt Ellie would have broken her promise to stay and walked out as soon as he mentioned Sarah was a ghost, had it not been for his mom nodding her head in agreement with what he said and interjecting comments into the story.

When Liam and his mom grew silent, their story told, Ellie exhaled. "Wow. What do we need to do now?"

"We?" Liam asked. "You don't need to get involved in this nightmare."

"For one thing, I already am involved. I helped you with the research, remember? For another thing, Sarah is mad at you, so you messed up somewhere. You need an outsider's help. Like me."

"It's not a bad idea," Liam's mom agreed. "Another girl, around Sarah's age. It might help."

Liam closed his eyes, *I'm never going to win an argument with these two.* He opened them again and looked at Ellie, her eyes were wide and shiny as if this was the most exciting thing she'd ever done. "Alright, let's do it."

"Before we head back over there, what do we need?" Ellie asked. "Holy water? Ouija board? I've seen all of the *Paranormal Activity* movies."

Liam shook his again. "We don't need any of that. She's not a demon, and she talks quite freely in her own voice. I think we should just head over there. We don't need any of the goofy stuff."

"Sorry," Ellie said, offended. "I've never done this before. I'm not sure what to expect. I'm just trying to help."

They came up with the beginning of a plan: return to Whitehurst to calm Sarah down. They had no idea how they would reclaim their house once they got there, but Liam felt better doing something instead of just waiting at the hospital.

Pulling into the driveway, they spotted the silent and sleeping house, an exhausted giant.

"Maybe she left?" Liam's mom said, peering through the windshield.

"I doubt it. Based on what I know about her, she could be giggling while dancing down the hallway, or playing your music box, or figuring out how to blow up the house, but definitely not gone."

Before getting out of the car, Ellie turned to Liam and asked, "Okay, now what do we need to do?"

"I'm not sure. We're in uncharted territory. I've never needed to calm a ghost before."

"Well, I haven't either but I say we go inside the house and see what happens."

"I guess. But I think we should leave the front door open. We might need to make a quick escape, like we had to earlier tonight. Which makes me think; Mom, since you are the one who has a driver's license, why don't you stay in the car with it running so we can get out of here if we need to?"

"Oh, Liam. I couldn't let you do that. I can't send my child and his friend into a haunted house by themselves."

"But Mom, Sarah knows me, and Ellie is about her age. I think we stand a chance going in there ourselves. A third person would be overwhelming. Plus if anything bad happens, I promise we'll run out here as fast as we can and jump in the car."

Liam could tell by the look in his mother's eyes she was fighting herself. She wanted to protect them but what he said made sense.

"Please, Mom. I'd feel better knowing you were safe out here."

"Okay. You two promise you'll run if things get wacky in there?"

"Uh, I think they are already pretty wacky. But yeah, we promise we will run like the wind if we're in danger." Ellie nodded.

"Okay. You two go in and I'll keep the windows down and the car running."

Opening the car door, Ellie said in her best tough girl voice, "Let's do this thing."

Chapter 26

Liam and Ellie crept up the porch steps in the darkness of the early morning. Everything was eerily quiet: no birds singing, no frogs croaking, nothing moving in the trees. Just unsettling silence.

Liam's hand hesitated on the doorknob, waiting to see if anything would happen. When nothing did, he turned the knob. The door creaked on its hinges, like a door out of a horror movie. Liam cringed. He could feel Ellie's hand on his back, her warm breath on his neck. He relaxed slightly.

He opened the front door all the way, but didn't step across the threshold. He waited and listened. The house remained quiet. All of the alarms had stopped, the ghostly screams were over. He reached his hand around the door, fumbling for the light switch. Nothing happened when he flicked the switch. The power was still out.

"Sarah," Liam yelled. "Can I come in?"

Nothing.

"Do you have any candles?" Ellie asked.

"In the kitchen. But I'm not sure what's in the way between here and there."

"Not a problem." Ellie flipped open her cell phone. With the screen illuminated, there was enough light to find their way through the living room and into the kitchen.

Feeling around the kitchen drawers, Liam found the emergency candles and the matches right next to them. Despite the crazy circumstances, Liam smiled. Mom was always so well prepared.

Liam struck the match, bathing the kitchen in the soft yellow glow. He exhaled, not realizing he had been holding his breath. The kitchen was a mess. All of the cabinet doors and drawers were open, their contents spilled all over the floor.

The oppressive silence felt as if it were closing in around them. "What should we do now?" Ellie asked.

"The sun porch. Her mother's music box is in there, and I've contacted her there before. Plus we won't have to tackle the stairs in the dark."

Liam and Ellie made their way back through the kitchen, around the obstacles in the living room, and came to the open door to the sunroom. He remembered all of the doors slamming. Why was this one open? He didn't mention this to Ellie. If she became any more anxious, she'd be grabbing skin with her nails, not just his shirt sleeve. Liam's breathing started coming fast and shallow, every muscle in his body tensed up, ready for whatever came next.

Suddenly, the faint strains of the music box playing *Reynardine* began. Liam and Ellie's eyes met over the candlelight for a brief second. They had to cross through the room entrance now or they would lose their courage.

As soon as they entered the room, the temperature dropped.

"Sarah? Are you in here?" Liam asked.

"I am," she sniffled. They followed the sound of her quiet sobs.

Liam felt the tension coming off Ellie in waves. Still, she spoke. "Why are you crying?"

"Who are you?" Sarah stammered, caught off guard.

Stepping away from Liam and closer to the music box and the direction of Sarah's voice, Ellie answered, "I'm Ellie, Liam's friend. He asked me to help him when he was looking for the man who killed your family. I helped him then, and I want to help you now. What can we do for you? I can tell you're upset."

"Thank you for all your help," Sarah sniffed. "You've done enough. Now it's time for me to do something."

"What's that?" Liam asked, was the situation about to get violent again?

"I owe you an apology, Liam," Sarah said. "You were the first person in all these years who was willing to admit I was real. You granted my single wish this entire time: find out who murdered my family. When you did, I was caught off guard and angry. I should not have taken my anger out on you. Not only was Nat Greenly able to live a full life, but since he was related to you, I was angry when you were trying to make excuses for him, saying he was tormented and remorseful."

"But I didn't mean..." Liam interrupted.

Sarah ignored him and kept talking. "It didn't seem fair to me. So I became angry - very angry. I'm sorry. I didn't mean for your father to get hurt. The last thing I want is for another person to suffer from this tragedy. You cannot be held responsible for the sins of your forefather. It is finished." A shadow fluttered by the music box.

"What do you mean?" Ellie asked. "What's finished?"

"My time here. The man who murdered my family confessed to the crime. You two can share the confession with the town and clear my name. I can rest in peace now. Thank you."

Before Liam or Ellie could answer, the temperature in the room rose. Sarah's presence was gone. A huge weight was lifted from Liam's shoulders. Sarah was at peace, his family was safe, and Ellie didn't think he was crazy. It was turning out to be a good night after all.

As the music from the music box tinkled to a stop, the lights flickered and then came back on. Liam glanced over at Ellie. She was grinning from ear to ear.

"Why the smile?" he asked.

"I was just thinking, this is going to get us some awesome extra credit in Mr. Langford's class."

About the author:

Heather Hamel is an author, horse trainer, and teacher. While working her way through college to become a teacher, she discovered a passion for storytelling, while working as a ghost tour guide in the historic and haunted town of St. Augustine, Florida.

After teaching for a few years, Heather could not shake storytelling. Today, she teaches and tutors students with dyslexia, as well as finds time to write at 5:00 am. She has written on-line horse articles, two middle grade novels, and is currently working on a four book crypto-zoological series for her middle grade readers.

Website: https://HeatherHamel.com

Made in the USA
Charleston, SC
09 September 2014